SHATTERED

Kathleen Long

For Dan and Annie. Always.

PLEASE NOTE

There is a temptation, when rereleasing stories written twelve years earlier, to rewrite phrasing and language to fit today's style. In reissuing my original Body Hunters trilogy, I've chosen not to update for changes in either my writing or technology. My hope is that you'll enjoy these stories—written before there was a video camera on every corner and a smart phone with GPS in every pocket—just as they are.

Happy reading.

CAST OF CHARACTERS

Eileen Caldwell—She's come home to Pittsburgh in order to reconnect with her surviving brother. But when he vanishes mysteriously, she finds herself in a race to save her brother...and her life.

Kyle Landenburg—A member of the Body Hunters, he's traveled to Pittsburgh as part of the case. But will his undeniable attraction to Eileen result in far more than an undercover investigation?

Jack Caldwell—An investigator in the U.S. Attorney's office, he's just made the largest arrest of his career. So how can his sudden disappearance be explained, especially when he vanishes exactly as his brother did five years earlier?

Patrick O'Malley—A United States Attorney, he's lost a key member of his staff and a dear family friend. He vows to do whatever it takes to bring Jack home, but is there something he's not telling anyone?

Nicholas DiMauro—An international real estate guru, he claims his frequent trips to town are purely due to his love of professional baseball. Is he telling the truth? Or is the man involved in something far more sinister than a day at the ballpark?

Michael Downum—An informant to Jack and a past survivor of attempted kidnapping, she may be the clue to breaking the case wide open.

The Body Hunters—Will Connor, Maggie Connor, Rick Matthews, Lily Christides, Silvia Hellman, and Martin Booker. Dedicated to finding the victims and villains society has abandoned, they'll use every means necessary to locate Jack Caldwell. The Body Clock is ticking....

PROLOGUE

Rumor had it Jack Caldwell hadn't set foot on the Majestic Overlook during the past five years. Not since the *incident*, as the Producer liked to call Robert Caldwell's disappearance.

The Producer supposed there was irony in the fact the promise of new evidence in Jack's latest case would be enough to bring him running to a location that had never yielded evidence in one of his oldest cases—that of his own brother.

The Producer knew people well enough to read Caldwell's body language, so he watched the man standing at the overlook, as the Producer's vehicle pulled into the parking lot.

He rode in a large SUV, and the truck's tires punished the gravel beneath, crushing the stones into the mountain soil.

Caldwell's shoulders tensed then eased—the sign of a man consciously aware of the signals he emitted.

The Producer smiled.

He'd thought taking the younger Caldwell down

might leave a sour taste in his mouth, but now that the moment was at hand, he felt nothing close to remorse. Matter of fact, he felt relief—a great big heaping dose of relief, at that.

"Give me a few minutes alone." The Producer spoke the words to the other two men in the SUV with him —one his driver, one his drone. "Watch for my signal."

The leather loafers he'd worn provided lousy footing as he crossed to where Caldwell waited, and he silently cursed himself for not thinking ahead.

Splotches of red and green dotted the lush Pennsylvania countryside, marking the Pittsburgh area's descent into autumn. The early afternoon sun hung high in the sky above, and the powerful Majestic Rock creek roared below.

The Producer thought about how easy it would be to shove Caldwell over the overlook's railing and into the water's swift current or onto the jagged outcropping of rocks.

His palms itched as he closed the gap, but he tamped down the urge to give in to the impulse. After all, he'd never been one to indulge impulses.

Never.

No, he was a planner, a *producer*—a man who made things happen exactly as they should.

Right now, his planning called for an abduction. The Producer would allow Caldwell the chance to provide him with the information he wanted. Check that. The information he *needed*.

As loathe as he was to admit weakness, the missing documents served as just that—the Producer's weakness, a veritable Achilles' heel.

If Caldwell failed to deliver then Caldwell would cease to exist. The equation was a simple one.

Not another soul was in sight as the Producer came to a stop a few feet behind Caldwell. Things were going just as planned, right down to the lack of potential witnesses.

"You're late," Caldwell said without turning around.

The Producer pulled his weapon and aimed. "I always did like to make an entrance."

His voice affected Caldwell just as he'd suspected it would. Caldwell spun around, the afternoon breeze blowing his dark brown hair out of place.

Shock and disbelief registered on his features, the lines of his face more noticeable than they'd been the last time the two men had met.

Caldwell made no move to smooth his hair, no move to attack, no move to flee. Nothing.

Instead, he stared down the barrel of the gun and blinked, shoving his hands into his pockets as he'd always done when nervous. So much for being in control of his actions.

The Producer focused now, shoving away the enjoyment of watching Caldwell's stunned reaction. There was work to be done and not much time in which to do it.

Caldwell's mouth opened and shut, like a fish on the line. How appropriate. "How did you—? Where did you—? Why?"

Caldwell's last question might have affected the

Producer's heart, if he had any heart left to affect. Life had taken care of that possibility years earlier.

"Thanks for making this so easy for me." He waved his gun at the scenery, quickly realigning his aim at the furrowed brow between Caldwell's eyes. "I understand you're not a big fan of this place."

Angry red splotches fired in Caldwell's cheeks. "You son of a—"

"Now, now." The Producer made a tsking noise with his mouth. "There will be plenty of time for niceties later on. Right now, you and I are going to take a ride."

"I'm not going anywhere—"

The Producer dropped his aim to Caldwell's thigh and pulled the trigger.

Surprise flashed across the younger man's face, followed in quick succession by denial, shock, and fear. He sank to his knees, then onto his side, unable to speak or move.

"Don't worry," the Producer said. "You'll sleep for a while and be good as new when you wake up."

He signaled for his two companions, and their footfalls sounded at his side instantly.

"Get him into the car before the drug knocks him completely unconscious." He turned, starting for the car without waiting. "This way, if anyone sees us we can say he's got a drinking problem."

He had one hand on the door handle when he remembered the rest of what he needed to say. "Search his car. Bring me any paperwork. You know what to do with the rest."

The less evidence Jack Caldwell left behind, the better.

With any luck at all, he'd simply vanish into thin air, just like his big brother, Robert. The Producer dropped onto the passenger seat, slammed the door and laughed.

Caldwell should be so lucky.

CHAPTER ONE

Body Clock: 6:20

E ileen Caldwell sat in the Renaissance bar of the Grand Pittsburgh Hotel and stared at the myriad liquor bottles lined up against the leaded glass mirror. Old money.

The place reeked of old money.

She glanced around at her fellow Friday night revelers and thought again.

The bar and hotel might scream old money, situated as they were along the north side of town, but the establishment's clientele suggested anything but. Brash and beautiful, the crowd was as young as it was plentiful.

She leaned across the bar and signaled to Henry, the long-time bartender. "Are you sure he's usually here by now?"

Eileen's younger brother, Jack, had asked her to meet him here tonight. Over two hours ago, to be precise.

Henry nodded as he slid another glass of club soda in front of her. "By now he'd be well into his second scotch." He gave a shrug and a wink, his dark eyes twinkling. "Maybe he got a better offer."

Eileen rolled her eyes at the man she'd once chatted with every Friday night. Back in the days before her older brother Robert had gone missing. Back in the days when she and Jack and Robert had sat here every Friday night without fail, commiserating about work and politics and life in general.

Then everything had changed.

Eileen had run away after Robert's disappearance. She could admit that now.

But she'd finally come back. She'd come home. She'd been hoping the call from Jack had been a sign he'd chosen to forgive her for deserting him, for leaving him alone with the media and the memories.

She stole a glance at the empty barstool by her side, the one she kept defending from predatory moves by twenty-something corporate types.

Her heart sank.

Maybe Jack wasn't going to show after all. Maybe he'd decided she wasn't worth forgiving. Not yet.

She drew in a long, slow breath and took a sip of her drink. She wasn't giving up. Recent events had taught her family mattered, and Jack was all the family she had left.

She pushed away from the stool, nodded to a nearby group of young women in their best Friday night suits and slid a generous tip toward Henry.

"Thanks," she called out.

Henry reached for the bill, his fingertips brushing against hers. "Welcome home, Eileen."

Welcome home.

She let the words play through her mind as she made her way through the crowd toward the sidewalk outside. The lights of PNC Park sat dark across the Monongahela River and she stopped suddenly, turning back to study the bar.

For a split second, time slipped away. Eileen remembered the bar as it had been when she'd been a regular. Less trendy. More empty than full.

The image carried her back to the night five years earlier when she and Jack had waited for Robert for hours, just as she'd waited for Jack tonight.

Robert had never shown up. Matter of fact, he'd never shown up anywhere ever again. His deserted car had been found an hour away, parked at the scenic Majestic Overlook.

A sudden urge to drive to the very spot threatened to overwhelm her, but she shoved it away.

What if Jack had reached out not to welcome her back, but to tell her he was neck-deep in some sort of trouble? A case more dangerous than usual?

As employees of the United States Attorney's office and specialized task forces, both he and Robert had been involved in many dangerous cases.

What if he hadn't stood her up by choice? What if something had gone horribly wrong?

Eileen was letting her imagination get the best of her, and she knew it.

Jack had just wrapped up one of the biggest arrests of his career. Successful convictions would shut down a major arm of the Basso crime family.

Pride welled inside her, but was edged away instantly by dread. Why couldn't one of her brothers have chosen a safer career? Like her career?

She laughed to herself. Both Jack and Robert would have been driven half-mad at the prospect of dealing with the ins and outs of hotel management.

A cab cruised slowly past, but Eileen decided to make the twenty-minute walk back to the small four-square she'd owned for years.

It was a gorgeous September night. Crisp and clear. Her favorite time of year in the city.

Besides, as far as she was concerned, a long walk in Pittsburgh was one of life's little pleasures.

The sounds and smells of the town she loved filled her, completed her, and she was struck again by how much she'd missed home during the years she'd lived in the Caribbean, on Isle de Cielo.

A couple strolled past, headed in the opposite direction, laughing and talking, and Eileen smiled. A perfect night.

But the shiver that danced down her spine suggested otherwise, as did the growing sensation of dread churning inside her.

She plucked her cell phone from her purse and speed-dialed Jack's number. Again.

The call clicked into voice mail instantly, just as her previous calls had done. He'd turned his phone off for some reason.

The chill in her spine reached around the base of

her neck and squeezed. Eileen quickened her pace, suddenly wanting to be nowhere but home.

Jack would undoubtedly have a good explanation in the morning about why he'd stood her up tonight, but in the meantime she was in for a sleepless night.

Not knowing where Jack might be had brought the past crashing into the present. She found herself consumed by a question that had haunted the corners of her mind for the past five years.

Where was her brother?

Only this time, the missing brother was Jack. And this time, Eileen had no intention of going anywhere until she got an answer, and put the discord in her mind to rest.

KYLE LANDENBURG woke in a cold sweat, wanting nothing more than to attribute the knot inside his gut to the overly spicy pizza he'd eaten too late the night before, but he knew better.

He'd had the dream again.

A jumble of flashing images and sounds, shadows and light. A figure without a face. A woman, perhaps? Fighting for her life?

He couldn't be sure, but this was the second time in the past week he'd had the vision. He was man enough to admit that's what the images were.

He wasn't man enough, however, to dwell on the possibilities of what those images might mean.

He'd never asked for the overly sensitive intuition he possessed. Matter of fact, if he could lose the skill tomorrow, he wouldn't waste a moment missing the ability after it was gone.

He reached for his cell phone where it sat on his nightstand, and pressed the display button. Five-fifteen. Almost four straight hours of sleep. A new record.

Kyle swung his legs over the side of the bed and reached for a sweatshirt from the chair next to his closet. He slid the worn cotton over his head then pulled on a pair of sweatpants. He clipped his phone to his waistband before he headed for the front door of his apartment.

There was nothing like a predawn run along the damp streets of Seattle to wake a man and clear his head.

The visions from his dream flashed through his mind's eye once more, and Kyle thought for a moment about trying to write them down, describe them, preserve them in case he might need them should their meaning become clear.

Instead, he shoved them away, far inside the odd workings of his brain. The visions had never done him much good in the past. He didn't expect them to start now.

Sure, his intuition had facilitated his work with The Body Hunters, but the visions? The visions were nothing more than incoherent flashes of shapes and sounds.

He pushed outside and the brush of damp air against his face slowly uncoiled the tension knotted inside him.

Nothing replaced sound mental and physical conditioning for keeping a man sharp. Combine that with smart teamwork—like Kyle's work with The Body Hunters—and life was good.

Even so, he remained ever vigilant, ever on guard.

He'd learned long ago to remain prepared for anything and everything.

If a man didn't learn to do that, sooner or later he'd find himself blindsided. Stung by the big, bad world outside when he least expected it.

Kyle had been stung once. He had no intention of being stung again.

His cell phone beeped to signal an incoming call and he instantly recognized the number—Will Connor, Body Hunters codirector.

"We got a hit on a cold case out of Pittsburgh."

Kyle slowed to a walk and focused on Will Connor's voice.

"Robert Caldwell."

Eileen Caldwell's older brother.

Kyle knew the case inside out. His research had bordered on obsession during the months since he'd met Eileen on Isle de Cielo. "Found his body?"

In the silence that followed, Kyle pictured Will shaking his head as clearly as if he stood before him instead of being on the other end of a phone call. The two had worked together for years, and understood each other's every move.

"Younger brother's car was found abandoned in the same spot where the older brother went missing. The local response triggered the hit on our system."

"Signs of struggle?" Kyle straightened, the images

from last night's dream replaying through his mind.

Could the vision have been some sort of a warning?

"My source in Pittsburgh says it's too soon to tell, but the press is all over this one. History repeats itself, et cetera."

"Eileen?" Kyle spoke the name softly.

"Maggie's trying to reach her now. I'll keep you posted."

Will's wife Maggie had struck up a friendship with Eileen during the Cielo investigation.

Apparently they'd remained in touch even after the team's return to Seattle. "Are you sending the team?" Kyle asked.

"I haven't yet made that determination."

But Kyle knew Will better than that.

During the Cielo case, Eileen had been instrumental in helping The Body Hunters rescue Jordan Connor, Will and Maggie's daughter. Kyle would be surprised if Will wasted any time mobilizing the team.

"If you need me—" Kyle hesitated, swallowing down an uncharacteristic knot of emotion, unsure as to how he intended to finish the sentence.

He'd known Eileen for a matter of days, but the woman had left her mark on him.

Simply being near her had flipped an internal switch Kyle had thought long dead. He'd vowed years earlier to never again become involved emotionally, no matter how much his gut protested otherwise.

Walking away from Eileen at the end of the Cielo investigation had been the smart thing to do, but would he be able to stay away now that she might need the team? Might need him?

"I'll be in touch," Will said before he ended the call.

Kyle picked up his pace, resuming his run. Yet every step he took did nothing to ease the tension coiling anew inside him, winding tighter and tighter.

WHEN THE PHONE rang a little after eight the next morning, Eileen's gut caught. In the split second before she reached for the receiver, she knew the news wouldn't be good.

A sense of foreboding had overwhelmed her sometime during the night, as if she expected this call, expected bad news.

As soon as her caller spoke, she knew her darkest fear had been realized.

Patrick O'Malley's voice filtered across the phone line as clearly as it had five years earlier. "They've found Jack's car, apparently abandoned."

The anticipation of Patrick's next words wrapped around Eileen's heart and squeezed. She reached for the nightstand with her free hand, gripping the carved wooden edge to steady herself.

"Where?" She forced the word through a fog of disbelief and denial.

Patrick might be one of the most powerful men in Pittsburgh, the United States Attorney for Western Pennsylvania, but he was also one of the Caldwell family's oldest friends. His hesitation told Eileen everything she needed to know.

"At the overlook."

The overlook?

"Majestic?" Eileen's stomach pitched sideways and rolled.

Each year thousands of people stood atop the scenic overlook, studying the rocky outcroppings below, but Jack hated the location.

They both did.

He would never go back there. Not without a very good reason.

She sank from the edge of the bed to the floor, her knees hitting the wooden planks with an unforgiving thud. "And Jack?"

"Driver's door was found open. There's no trace of him, Eileen." Another hesitation. Another roll of Eileen's stomach. "I'm headed there now."

"He was supposed to meet me last night," she said softly, her brain refusing to wrap itself around Patrick's words.

"Let's not jump to conclusions. For all we know he broke down there and walked home. Maybe he forgot to lock the car."

Patrick, ever the cold, unfeeling voice of reason.

Eileen shook her head. "You know that's not true."

But Patrick's tone never wavered, his voice remaining steady and confident. "I'll call you as soon as I know anything more."

A few moments later, Eileen stood on her small back patio, letting the morning air wash over her like a cold shower. The soft scent of her wildflower garden typically soothed her, but today the blossoms smelled cloyingly sweet, at odds with the bitter reality tumbling through her.

Jack had gone missing.

She wrapped her arms around her waist and analyzed every word of her conversation with Patrick O'Malley.

The man had been part of her family for as long as she could remember. Even though years younger than her grandfather, the two men had been great friends, and Patrick had been part of every family gathering. Every communion. Every confirmation. Every funeral.

She'd never felt fully at ease with Patrick, yet he'd been a fixture in her life, in her family's life.

For that, she had to trust him.

He was loyal. And although he never said as much, she knew he cared about her and about her brothers.

A chill sliced through her and she pulled the neck of her robe more tightly to her throat. She and her brothers had lost their parents years ago, as young children.

They'd buried their grandmother fifteen years ago, their grandfather seven years ago. Robert had disappeared two years after that, and now Jack...

Eileen shook her head, turning to step back into the warmth of her kitchen and the waiting pot of coffee.

For all she knew, Jack was fine. Maybe Patrick was right about the car. Perhaps it had broken down and Jack was home asleep in bed, even though her calls to him last night had all gone unanswered.

Maybe he'd met someone.

Perhaps he'd done something unpredictable like

race off to Las Vegas for a romantic weekend. Her heart sank disbelievingly at the thought.

Neither of her brothers had ever done an unpredictable thing in their lives. They weren't wired that way. Jack was the worst offender of the two.

For as long as Eileen could remember, Jack's life had been a picture of schedule and consistency. Eileen, on the other hand, was as rebellious as her brother was regimented.

Her thoughts flashed back to the recent years she'd spent on Isle de Cielo and her work there as a resort manager. Life had been good, unpredictable and carefree, but empty. Very empty.

She'd come home to face the past, to come to terms with Robert's disappearance. She'd come home to face the ghosts from which she'd run away.

Images and faces raced through her mind. The men and women she'd met during her final days on the island.

The Body Hunters.

A group of private individuals with a secret, shared cause—finding the missing, be they victims or villains.

The Body Hunters team had taken her into their confidence and there she'd witnessed dedication as she'd never witnessed dedication before.

Their passion for their work was without equal. Their love and respect for each other without question. The fire in their eyes undeniable.

Their strength of conviction had inspired her to come home to Pittsburgh, to come home to her brother Jack.

She reached for her cell phone where it sat charging on her kitchen counter and scrolled through her contact list. She and Maggie Connor, wife of one of The Body Hunters founders, had become friends on Cielo.

Eileen knew local Pittsburgh law enforcement was more than capable of handling a missing person's case, yet she needed something more. She needed to know every possible action was being taken, and she needed to be part of the solution.

If she could convince Maggie she needed the team's help, maybe, just maybe, they'd come to Pittsburgh. And then Eileen would know she'd done everything possible to bring Jack home.

Eileen glanced at the clock on the far wall. Eight-fifteen. Only five-fifteen in Seattle.

Another Body Hunters team member's face popped into her mind. This one male, gentle and strong.

She hadn't spoken to Kyle Landenburg since the day they'd gone their separate ways, yet not a day passed in which he didn't cross her mind.

Surely he'd think her insane if she called him now and woke him to tell him her worst fears. Yet, for some reason, she was filled with a sense of knowing that Kyle, of all people, would understand her need to do her own investigating.

Eileen set the phone on the counter without making either call. Then she poured a cup of coffee and willed her mind to let go of the doomsday scenarios it had formulated.

The police had found Jack's car.

Yes, the door had been left open, but there was a chance Jack was fine, and a chance he was unharmed and safe somewhere.

But as she settled into a kitchen chair and waited for the phone to ring, hoped for Jack to call her, Eileen knew Jack wasn't fine at all.

She felt more alone than she had ever felt in her life.

Jack was missing from the same location where Robert's deserted car had been found years earlier.

Same location. Same situation.

Only this time, Eileen wasn't going to run away.

She pushed away from the chair, grabbed her phone and headed for her bedroom, determined to dress and get to the overlook as quickly as possible.

This time, she'd face reality head-on and she'd fight for her brother.

She'd find a way to bring Jack home. No matter what she had to do.

She dialed Jack's cell phone again, purely on instinct.

This time, the line rang.

Hope surged inside her, but the voice that answered shattered her every illusion.

"Where did you find the phone?" she asked Patrick.

"Discarded along the walkway above the river, as if someone intended to toss it out of sight."

Jack would never go anywhere without his cell phone. The phone was his lifeline to his work, his cases, his informants.

Silence beat across the line and held.

"What aren't you telling me?" Eileen asked, not

doing a thing to hide the despair in her voice.

"This is an active investigation scene. You know better than to ask me that."

For as long as she could remember, Patrick O'Malley had expected Eileen to accept his word as gospel. Her natural propensity for asking questions had been discouraged.

Apparently, some things never changed.

Well, that was too bad.

"Patrick."

Another silence greeted her sharp tone, yet this time, Patrick surprised her by answering.

"We found his laptop along the riverbank. The hard drive's gone."

Eileen winced. A raw wave of loss crashed through her.

"Just like Robert's," she said flatly.

"It's too soon to tell," Patrick answered. "I'll call you as soon as I know more."

But as far as Eileen was concerned, it wasn't too soon to tell.

Jack had vanished in an identical manner to the way in which Robert had vanished, and she'd be damned if she'd sit back and let local law enforcement handle a second brother's disappearance as offhandedly as they'd handled the first.

This time when she reached for the phone, she felt no hesitation. Jack needed help.

She needed help.

And she knew just where to find it.

CHAPTER TWO

Body Clock: 21:05

J ack Caldwell fought against the dense fog pulling him back toward unconsciousness even as he struggled to shake off the effects of the drug.

He blinked, the move serving only to blur his surroundings.

He blinked again, this time holding his eyes shut for the count of three before opening them slowly, letting his brain come to life.

The sight that greeted him sent his insides tumbling end over end.

He lay on a packed dirt floor, his joints and bones protesting the cold, hard earth. A lantern glowed dimly in the corner, illuminating dank, dark walls.

He struggled to his knees, but toppled immediately onto his side. His abductor's sedative refused to let go of its hold over Jack's brain signals.

No matter. He was young and he was in shape.

He'd work at kneeling until he succeeded. Then

he'd work at standing. And walking. And escaping.

The face of the man at the overlook flashed through Jack's mind—the eyes, once familiar, had morphed into those of a stranger, unrecognizable in their heartless intent.

The level set of the man's stare—and weapon—had hit Jack like a kick in the gut.

He'd taken one look at the other men and known he was about to be shot. That's when Jack had reached for his worry stone. He reached for it now, sliding his left hand into his pocket, but found the well-worn stone was gone.

Had he dropped it when he'd been hit? He could only hope that his assailant and the men with him had overlooked the oddly colored rock. Perhaps the stone would catch the eye of an investigator or responding officer. Perhaps someone would realize Jack hadn't dropped the stone by choice.

He knew the thought was a desperate one, but right now desperate was all he had.

Truth was, he'd hit the ground so quickly after impact, he had no idea what had become of the small stone.

The dart—he assumed he'd been hit with a dart —had delivered an immediate shock to his system, spreading its paralytic effects outward from the point of impact. He'd lost the use of his body almost instantly.

The last thing he remembered was being dumped into the back of an SUV by two large men.

How long had he been unconscious? Hours? Days?

He rolled up onto his knees once more, this time succeeding in holding his balance.

"Not as spry as you used to be, eh, Jack?"

Disbelief slid through him, just as it had back at the overlook. He turned to find his abductor standing in a narrow doorway.

Was this the man he'd once trusted completely?

"How could you do this?" Jack asked.

The other man merely shook his head, a sly smile spreading across his face. "The more accurate question would be, how could I not? You've been asking too many questions."

Jack frowned, his muddied brain unable to make sense of what he'd just heard.

The other man laughed, apparently reading the confusion on Jack's face.

"They'll look for me." Jack forced the words from his parched throat. "My car. My phone. My laptop. They're all at the overlook."

The other man pressed his lips into a tight line. "Your phone and laptop have been taken care of and your car..." He shrugged. "Let's just say the way you left your car at the overlook fits perfectly with suicide."

A knot of fear and dread seized Jack's throat and squeezed.

"That's right." The other man nodded. "You left a note back at your apartment. Short and sweet. No one will give your disappearance a second thought."

"No one will believe you. I was supposed to meet —" Jack left the sentence unfinished. He had no intention of pulling Eileen into this.

"You and I both know the police will believe whatever the evidence tells them." Jack's abductor closed the space between them and lifted one foot to Jack's shoulder. "Now then, you have something I need, and you're going to tell me exactly where to find it."

Jack studied the shoe—expensive leather, polished to a gleam, yet coated with a fine layer of dust.

The kind of shoes only a crook would wear, Jack's grandfather would have said. How right he would have been.

"You'll deliver," his abductor continued, giving a slight push with the sole of his shoe. "Or else I'll go after the one thing you've got left—your precious sister."

Jack toppled to the ground, anger and frustration seething inside him. "She's got nothing to do with what you want, and you know it."

The other man gave a shrug. "I know she came running back to Pittsburgh, and you're going to tell me why. Otherwise, I'll ask her myself."

"You wouldn't."

"I would." The man nodded, his lips twisting into a smirk.

As Jack lay on the unforgiving ground, the weight of the other man's shoe pressing into his ribs, he could think of only one thing.

The truth he'd uncovered during the past several months was so ugly, so surreal, he knew nothing he could say or do would save Eileen if this man was determined to go after her.

Even if Jack cooperated, his abductor would never rest if he suspected Eileen knew the truth.

There was only one thing that could save her now.

And that one thing was something she'd done beautifully for as long as Jack could remember.

She had to run—as fast and as far from Pittsburgh as she could.

And as his abductor delivered a swift kick to his ribs, Jack willed Eileen to do just that.

EILEEN HAD BEEN pacing back and forth along the length of her kitchen for hours, waiting for another call from Patrick.

He'd told her to sit tight, but sitting tight had never been something she'd done well. What she'd done best her entire life had been running—away from whatever conflict or heartache life had delivered.

This time would be different, no matter how loud and strong her flight instinct became.

She'd stay in Pittsburgh and face whatever it was that had happened to Jack, and she wouldn't be alone.

Maggie Connor had phoned at the exact moment Eileen had reached for the phone to ask for help.

The Body Hunters were on their way, and Eileen couldn't be more relieved. Even more than the moral support she knew the team would bring her, they'd bring their expertise and their fast work.

She'd seen examples of both during their recent Isle de Cielo investigation.

If a way existed to locate Jack alive and bring him home, The Body Hunters would find it.

Kyle Landenburg's face flashed through her mind once more, and she came to a stop, freezing midpace.

Would the gentle giant of a man be part of the team handpicked for this case? Her brother's case?

She'd know soon enough. Maggie had promised to call once the team was on the ground in Pittsburgh.

The ring of the doorbell cut Eileen's thoughts short and she raced down the home's center hall.

Patrick stood waiting outside on the steps.

Eileen read the pain in his face and instantly feared the worst. "Did you find him?"

Patrick stepped inside and shook his head. "We found a note."

"A note?" Her heart pounded in her ears.

"A suicide note."

The bottom fell out of Eileen's stomach, and Patrick grasped her arm to steady her.

He pulled a sheet of paper from his pocket. "It's a copy," he said as he handed her the sheet.

Eileen kept her eyes locked on his as she took the paper, then held her breath before she dropped her gaze to the photocopied words, sprawled in the handwriting she knew so well.

Too tired to go on. I'm sorry for the pain.

"He would never write this." She spoke the words in barely more than a whisper, unable to believe what she was seeing.

Another brother gone. Another suicide. It couldn't

be. There had to be a mistake. *There had to be.*

"Maybe someone held a gun to his head?" She barely recognized her own voice, knowing she sounded as crazed as she suddenly felt.

Patrick steered her toward the kitchen, encouraging her to sit down. Yet she dodged the chair he offered, moving instead toward the kitchen's island, leaning into the solid object for support.

"The investigative team found the note on his desk, in an envelope with your name on it," he explained. "I'm sorry."

Eileen read the words again, concentrating on their meaning.

She frowned. "He would never say this. He loved his life. Loved his work." She lifted her focus to Patrick's face. For once the man's features showed lines of strain, lines of grief. "You've known him since he was a kid. This isn't him."

"I have my entire staff in for questioning now. We'll soon know whether or not he'd changed recently. Whether or not he'd become depressed."

Depressed.

Hadn't she and Jack both been depressed at some point or another during the time since their older brother had fallen off the face of the earth? How could they not be? But Jack…Jack wouldn't have taken his own life. It wasn't possible.

"Eileen?"

Patrick's voice broke through her thoughts.

The older man leaned close, his eyes never leaving hers. "Had he mentioned seeing a doctor? Taking any medication? Anything?"

Maybe he would have if they'd spoken more than a handful of times in recent years.

She shook her head. "I don't know. We didn't talk about those things."

Truth was, they didn't talk at all. That's why she'd been so looking forward to last night, before her world tipped on its side.

Eileen pressed her lips together, biting back the sob that threatened to burst from her throat. She would not cry. She would not grieve. Jack had not killed himself, just as Robert had not killed himself years earlier.

What in the hell was going on?

She shook her head, waving the copy of the letter in the air. "This is a lie."

Patrick captured her hands in his exactly as he'd done the day he'd broken the news that her parents had been killed along a lonely stretch of highway.

She'd run that day—deep into the wooded country-side surrounding her family's farm. Patrick had been the first to find her, the first to talk to her. Just as he was the first to be with her now.

"You worked with him every day." She searched Patrick's face. "Surely you don't need to ask your staff if he was depressed. Did he seem depressed to you?"

The older man hesitated a moment too long. The lines around his dark eyes deepened as he winced. "Matter of fact, he did."

He squeezed her hands then broke contact, taking a backward step, distancing himself—as always—both emotionally and physically.

"I'll see every piece of this investigation through to the end." He spoke quickly and methodically, all signs of caring gone from his eyes and expression. "We'll start with verifying this handwriting, but you have to prepare yourself for the possibility Jack wrote this note then took his own life."

Eileen flinched at the harshness of Patrick's words. Tears, angry tears, swam in her vision. "And you believe that? You believe this? You honestly think he'd kill himself? When he'd just cracked the case of a lifetime?"

She crumpled the letter in her hand.

"Eileen—"

"No." She turned her back on Patrick and his cold acceptance of her brother's fate. She splayed her hands atop the cool granite counter top and willed her body to stop trembling. "I refuse to believe this. He's not dead."

The older man made no further move to comfort her. "I'm only asking you to prepare yourself, that's all."

Eileen squeezed her eyes shut momentarily before she turned to glare at Patrick. "You're asking me to believe my brother's dead, and I won't do it."

She pointed to the crumpled sheet of paper. "If you're so sure he killed himself, why didn't you bring me the original? Why protect it?"

One corner of his mouth lifted, yet the rest of his face remained dispassionate. "I believe in keeping investigations nice and neat."

Just like he'd always kept his life.

While Patrick had been an ever-present face at her family's life events, he'd never been what she would have called warm or affectionate. His cool, analytical mind had been custom-made for his line of work—for the United States Attorney's office.

He turned toward the door. "I'll check back in later. Sit tight. Try to get some rest."

But Eileen had no intention of sitting or resting or accepting what she'd just been told. The Body Hunters were on their way.

As soon as she got the call with the location of the safe house they'd be using in her brother's case, she'd be on the move.

Together, they'd find Jack and bring him home... alive. They had to.

The alternative was too unbearable to consider.

KYLE KICKED BACK in his seat as The Body Hunters jet sped toward Pittsburgh.

Will Connor moved toward the front of the cabin and lowered the case board from the plane's ceiling. The man had run every Body Hunters case from the team's Seattle bunker for years. Recent events had brought him back into the field.

He'd faked his death years earlier to save the lives of his wife and infant daughter, but all that was behind him now, his old enemy dead and gone. Will's wife, Maggie, had joined the team, dedicating herself to the work her husband and the team's cofounder, Rick Matthews, had funded through hard work and the sale of their own business years earlier.

Today, it was Rick who had stayed behind and Will who led the team.

Kyle straightened in his seat.

The team had assembled in record time. Will and Maggie. Kyle. Silvia Hellman and Martin Booker.

Silvia, a retired librarian, boasted an uncanny ability to work her research and computer skills for the good of every mission. Martin's skill at manipulating data and developing electronic gadgets had served the team well on many occasions since the young man had joined them.

Will pointed to two photos, one of Robert Caldwell, the second of Jack Caldwell. Kyle recognized them instantly from his own research into Eileen's family history.

"With the exception of Martin, you all know Eileen Caldwell from our time on Isle de Cielo," Will explained. "These are her brothers, both part of the United States Attorney's office in Pittsburgh."

He pointed to the first headshot. "Robert vanished from the Majestic Overlook north of Pittsburgh five years ago. His car and cell phone were found deserted. His laptop was found in the rushing water below, minus its hard drive." He met each team member's eyes in turn. "Robert's body was never found."

Will stepped to one side, giving the team a moment to digest the information then he pointed to Jack's photo.

"Eileen's younger brother Jack has spent the past five years searching for his brother while carrying on

Robert's legacy within the United States Attorney's office.

"While local law enforcement declared Robert's disappearance a suicide and have presumed the elder Caldwell brother to be dead, neither Jack nor Eileen ever accepted that determination.

"In the meantime, Jack recently made the first in a series of arrests planned to cripple the Basso crime family, zeroing in on their illegal slot and poker machine operations through the Commonwealth of Pennsylvania."

Silvia straightened in her seat, pointing to Robert's photo. "Didn't Robert's disappearance follow a large-scale arrest also?"

Will nodded. "Yes. His investigation also involved the Basso family, but concerned their illegal drug trade. The timing and circumstances of both disappearances are beyond eerie in their similarities."

"What happened to the Basso case Robert had been spearheading?" Martin asked.

"It fell apart in court." Will gave a tight nod then redirected the focus to Jack Caldwell's disappearance. "According to preliminary information coming out of Pittsburgh, Jack Caldwell's car was found early this morning. The driver's door had been left ajar. His cell phone had been tossed from a nearby pedestrian path but was not destroyed. His laptop, however, had been hurled to the riverbank below, hard drive missing."

Martin let out a long, low whistle. "I've never heard of two cases being so similar."

"I don't believe any of us have," Will replied.

"That's why we're going."

Maggie, Will's wife, pushed to her feet and faced the group, tucking her long, blond hair behind her ears.

The woman who had spent most of her adult life hiding from the world had embraced life in recent months. Jack Caldwell's disappearance had visibly infused her with a sense of purpose and determination Kyle had witnessed in her once before, during the team's search for Maggie's daughter.

"Eileen Caldwell is a friend to this team. We need to treat her as such."

Silence stretched through the small cabin, as her words hit their mark.

"There's one more thing," Maggie said. "Just before we left the airport, we received word that a suicide note had been found."

"Handwriting?" Martin asked.

"We don't have any more specific information," Maggie answered.

Martin's eyes narrowed. "I need to get my hands on a copy, and a copy of another piece of correspondence we know Jack wrote."

Will shook his head. "Shouldn't be a problem. I'm sure Eileen will cooperate in every way possible."

"First steps?" Silvia asked.

Will grabbed a pen and jotted notes on a dry erase board as he spoke.

"We'll start by combing the scene of the disappearance, Jack's home, and his office. We'll interview his staff and review every detail we can on the Basso indictments.

"Was there someone he wasn't able to arrest?" he continued. "Are there outstanding warrants? Are there pieces of that particular puzzle that don't fit? Who gains by Jack's disappearance? Were there other cases on his plate recently?"

Kyle studied each team member's face—all focused and intense. If any group of people could get to the bottom of Jack Caldwell's disappearance, they could.

"Let's look beyond the obvious," Will continued. "According to Eileen, her younger brother was a creature of habit. What made him break his pattern? And why?"

"Where will we be staying?" Martin asked.

"Secluded location outside city limits, but close enough to the crime scene to make coming and going routine," Will answered. "I've given specific instructions on outfitting the case room, and I trust everything will be to your liking."

Will looked at his watch. "We land in less than thirty minutes. Let's take that time to grab some quiet time and recharge. We're going to hit the ground running on this one. From here on out, sleep will be a luxury."

Quiet fell across the cabin, but Kyle's mind refused to stop working the case possibilities.

Excitement built inside him, as it did at the start of every case, but this time, the sense of anticipation he felt seemed heightened. Why?

Because of the case itself? Or because of the woman he was about to see?

Eileen.

Kyle shoved the image of the attractive brunette deep into the recesses of his brain. He forced himself to focus on the case board, on the photos of Jack and Robert Caldwell, on the list of action steps to be taken.

He'd learned long ago never to let emotions distract him from a case. Yet try as he might, he couldn't stop the tangle of anticipation and excitement churning inside him.

Yet the team, the case, and the welfare of Eileen's brother depended on his objectivity. He had no choice but to keep his thoughts and actions under control.

And he would.

He'd do his job in Pittsburgh and then he'd return to his life in Seattle. He and Eileen would go their separate ways once again.

Giving thought to any other outcome was a waste of focus and energy, and Kyle had never been a man to waste either.

He wasn't about to start now.

CHAPTER THREE

Body Clock: 27:45

Eileen cranked on her car's ignition then reached for her GPS unit, entering the address Maggie had given her for the safe house. The satellite system worked its magic and began delivering instructions a few moments later.

Forty minutes outside of the city, she followed the unit's command to turn onto a heavily wooded dirt path and seriously wondered when it was she'd begun trusting computers over good old-fashioned maps.

The lost signal message winked at her from the GPS screen, vanishing only momentarily when she emerged from beneath the heavy tree canopy.

The path took her deeper into the heavy foliage and the GPS system proved worthless. She breathed a sigh of relief when a large log house appeared at the end of the lane, flanked by a pond and a barn.

Four late-model black sedans sat parked to one side

of the barn and anxiety flickered through her. Either she'd found The Body Hunters safe house, or she'd stumbled upon an organized crime meeting.

She pulled her car to a stop beneath what looked to be a two-hundred-year-old oak tree, shooting her GPS unit a frown as it continued to blink its lost signal message at her.

"Eileen!"

Maggie's voice reached through the car windows and relief flooded through Eileen. She was out of the car and in the other woman's embrace in a matter of seconds.

"Thank you for coming." Gratitude hung heavy in Eileen's voice, and she hadn't realized until that instant just how much the team's support meant to her.

Maggie pushed her to arm's length. "I wouldn't be anywhere else and you know it. Same goes for the team."

A new light shimmered in her friend's pale eyes, a twinkle that hadn't been there when they'd first met on Cielo.

Eileen imagined rediscovering a love thought long-lost could do that for a woman. Maggie had not only found out her husband Will was very much alive, but they'd also rebuilt their family and their marriage, starting with the successful rescue of their daughter Jordan from a Body Hunters team imposter.

"You look...radiant." Eileen gave Maggie's hand a squeeze.

Maggie grinned and pressed a finger to her lips. "No one on the team knows, but I have reason to glow."

She patted her abdomen gently. "Seven months to go."

"Good to see you, Eileen." Will's voice interrupted the happy laugh the two women shared, snapping Eileen's thoughts away from Maggie's news and back to the reason her friends had traveled cross-country. "Team's waiting inside."

Maggie captured Eileen's face in her hands. "We'll find Jack. You'll see."

The genuine friendship and concern in Maggie's voice and touch sent tears springing to life in Eileen's eyes. She hadn't yet cried for Jack, and she wasn't about to now.

She blinked the moisture away and nodded. "Let's get this show on the road."

She followed Maggie and Will into the house, and was taken aback by the warm interior. She hadn't expected something so homey, and yet she knew she shouldn't be surprised.

On Cielo, the team's safe house had been a beautifully decorated beachfront bungalow—complete with a fully outfitted, high-tech bunker.

This house proved to be no different. While the smell of freshly brewed coffee filled the air and a roaring fire crackled and popped in an oversized brick fireplace, the team met in a large room down a set of steps.

Three separate computer screens glowed and several charts and lists hung from the room's walls.

If she didn't know better, Eileen would have thought the team had been in place for days instead of minutes.

Silvia Hellman pushed away from one of the computer workstations, her eyes crinkling with a mixture of pleasure and sympathy. She took Eileen's hands in hers, her kind touch infusing Eileen with strength. "So good to see you again, I just wish it were under different circumstances."

"Likewise," Eileen answered.

A younger man worked diligently at a side table, setting out an array of tools and gadgets. He looked up, his black glasses askew on his young face. He couldn't be more than twenty-two or twenty-three.

"I don't believe you've met Martin Booker, the newest member of our team," Will explained. Eileen and Martin shook hands, each smiling a silent greeting.

"Lily won't be with us on this mission," Will continued, "but I'm sure you'll remember Kyle Landenburg."

Eileen swallowed down the knot of emotion tightening in her throat. She didn't have to see the man to feel his presence. She turned slowly and there he stood, all six foot four of intense male strength.

He'd apparently been upstairs and had followed Eileen and Maggie down into the case room, his moves silent, as usual.

He greeted her with nothing more than a nod, his features unreadable, yet his eyes offered a brief glimpse into the man inside, a peek at the warmth and caring he kept so carefully hidden.

Was he happy to see her? Had he thought of her during the past few months?

She knew the thoughts were crazy, considering today's circumstances, and yet she couldn't seem to shake the questions from her mind.

He stepped toward her, lifting one hand as if he might touch her arm or hand as a gesture of comfort and welcome, but then he shifted, reaching to offer her a chair.

The moment and its potential were lost.

Eileen and Maggie sat side by side, and Kyle moved away to lean against the wall. Will stepped toward a handwritten list, no doubt prepared by the team in preparation for their arrival.

"We have some action steps planned," Will explained. "But first, I'd like you to tell us everything that's happened so far. From the beginning."

Forty-five minutes later, Eileen had detailed everything she knew, starting with her time spent at the Renaissance bar the night before.

She'd forgotten how intense the team's case room meetings had been in Cielo, at least the small portion she'd witnessed.

The Body Hunters were cautious about letting outsiders catch a glimpse of their inner workings, and she couldn't blame them. She was grateful they considered her one of their own, and thankful they'd come all the way across country when she'd needed them.

"We need to start tonight." The sound of Kyle's voice sent her insides tightening.

The man hadn't said one word during the entire

time she'd talked, but the sound of his voice now brought flashes of their time on Cielo rushing back.

His strength. His conviction. His intensity.

He affected her senses now as he had then, and she fought against it, wanting to keep her head sharp, clear, free of an unwanted attraction.

"The bar?" Will asked.

Kyle nodded. "And the bartender."

"Very well." Will pointed to Kyle. "You and Eileen see what you can find out. The rest of us will get things rolling here."

Kyle and Will were right, of course.

Based on Eileen's memory and the two hours she'd spent at the Renaissance bar the night before, Jack had felt more at home there than anywhere else. The bartender, at least, knew him as a person, not as a criminal attorney. The bar was as good a place as any to start the hunt for clues.

"Take this before you leave." Martin scrambled for a tiny object, handing it to Kyle. "Navigation system. You never know when you might need it. It's also a tracking device. Keep it in your pocket when it's not in use and we'll always know where you are."

Kyle lifted one pale brow.

"Martin loves his gadgets," Maggie said softly. "But they do come in handy." She gave Eileen another hug before the group meeting broke. "Why don't you pack a bag while you're in town and stay here?"

"What if Jack tries to find me?" Even as Eileen spoke the words, she knew the chances of Jack trying to reach out to her were minimal. Either he'd committed suicide, as Patrick had suggested, or he'd met with foul play.

Maggie gave her hand a squeeze. "You think about it." She shot a knowing glance at Kyle, who now stood in close conversation with Will. "I'd tell you to be careful, but I have a very strong suspicion Kyle would never let a thing happen to you."

NIGHT HAD SETTLED solidly over the city of Pittsburgh by the time Eileen and Kyle headed for downtown. Kyle drove one of the team sedans, but hadn't said a word since they'd left the safe house.

"Shall we try the new GPS unit?" she asked, grasping at something with which to break the silence. "Maybe it works better than the one in my car."

Kyle nodded and pulled the unit from his pocket. So much for conversation.

Eileen set the unit for the Grand Pittsburgh's address then let her thoughts take over as she stared out at the approaching city skyline.

Eileen wasn't sure if what she felt whenever Kyle was near was attraction or intimidation.

Around him, she experienced a heightened sense of awareness. Sights and sounds and scents all seemed larger and sharper. The man himself presented a presence far and above that of most every other man she'd ever met.

The sense of power he exuded went beyond his towering height and the strength of his build. His countenance hinted at something that went far deeper. A past wound. A loss. An experience.

Eileen sensed that in Kyle's life there had been an event so powerful it had shaped him, altering his internal makeup forever.

They'd never spoken of their personal lives. Yes, she'd told him briefly about Robert's disappearance, but she'd never provided details. They'd never crossed the line from casual conversation to intimate.

Would they ever?

Her pulse quickened.

"Eileen?" The deep rumble of his voice slashed through her thoughts as he pulled the car to the curb. "We're here."

The lights of PNC Park blazed from across the river, and across the street well-dressed patrons zipped in and out of the bar's entryway.

"So we are," she answered. She'd been so lost in thought that most of the drive from the safe house hadn't registered.

"I'll follow your lead." Kyle cut the ignition and leaned past her to peer at the hotel architecture. "Upscale." He sat back, pressed a hand to her arm and locked stares. "Ready?"

The touch of his hand to her arm sent a jolt through her system, bringing every nerve ending to attention. She nodded.

A few moments later, they'd made their way through the crowd and secured a spot at the bar. Eileen sat on a stool while Kyle stood guard beside her.

Kyle's presence didn't go unnoticed by Henry. "What can I get for you and your friend?"

Kyle ordered two soda pops then angled his body to study the room.

Henry said nothing about Jack as he turned to fill the order, but that changed the moment he returned.

"I'm sorry for your trouble."

"Thanks," Eileen whispered.

"I can't picture him doing something like this. Not on purpose." "That's why we...I...wanted to talk to you."

"Shoot."

"Had he changed, Henry?" she asked.

The bartender frowned, ignoring a customer at the end of the bar who called out for some service. "A bit more reserved, but nothing drastic, no."

Jack had never been someone anyone would have called reserved. "Did you get the sense it was his work?"

Henry thought for a moment then gave a quick nod. "He never talked about specifics, but I got the sense he was under a lot of pressure."

"Did he ever meet anyone here?"

Henry pursed his lips. "The occasional female, but no one regular."

That was Jack. Married to his job. He used to joke that he'd been married to the *mob*, he'd worked so hard to break apart the Basso family.

If Eileen had stayed in touch with her brother, she'd know what had been happening in his life instead of sitting here in a downtown bar interviewing the bartender.

"I always wondered why he kept a regular reservation here."

Eileen blinked. She'd been so lost in self-recrimination that she'd missed whatever it was Henry had said.

Based on Kyle's body language, the bartender had said something worthy of taking notice.

"Jack kept a regular reservation here?" Confusion swirled inside her. Her brother lived but a few blocks from the hotel. Why on earth would he keep a room here?

"Not Jack." Henry shook his head, cutting his eyes to the side and back as if he were afraid someone might overhear. "*Robert*. That's what I was saying. Jack had grown obsessed with Robert's disappearance. Suddenly, Robert's past was as important to Jack as his work at the U.S. Attorney's office."

Beside her, Eileen sensed tension building inside Kyle.

"Thanks," Kyle said flatly as he tossed a twenty onto the bar then steered Eileen away.

"What are you doing?"

He was pulling her away now? Just when they'd fallen into potentially useful information?

But Kyle didn't answer her as he guided her effortlessly through the crowd and out onto the street. "He knows something more than what he's saying. And we need more information than he'll have."

"Which means?"

He pulled his phone from his pocket. "Which means we tell Silvia to work her magic and get us inside the hotel system. We need to know when your brother Robert stayed here and why. And we need the name of every guest who stayed here at the same time."

"You think Jack uncovered something about Robert's past that led to his own disappearance?"

His expression cooled, as if he wanted to keep her from whatever it was he was thinking. "Call it a hunch."

"A hunch?"

Eileen blinked, pulling her arm free of Kyle's touch, as much as part of her wanted to stay connected to the man's heat and strength. "Robert's been gone for five years, Kyle. We'll never find those records."

And then Kyle did something Eileen had never seen him do before. He smiled.

The move lit his face so brightly she momentarily lost her breath. She swallowed down her surprise and refocused.

Robert. Jack. Meetings and hotel rooms. Hacking into hotel databases.

If Eileen had any intention of finding out the truth, she needed to give less thought to Kyle's smile and more thought to the puzzle pieces in play.

"After all—" Kyle's grin deepened "—it seems to me you'd be just the person to know where to look when it comes to hotel record-keeping."

She hadn't yet found a job since her return to Pittsburgh, but Kyle was right. She'd spent her career working her way up through the ranks of hotel and resort management. She, of all people, should know how to access information.

She blew out a sigh and nodded. "You're right. Let's go."

They'd barely driven a block when exhaustion hit Eileen like a brick wall, folding in on her after the long hours of waiting, worrying, and disbelief.

She leaned against the passenger door and Kyle noticed immediately. "You need to slow things down for a bit."

She studied him, grateful for his concern. "I'm okay."

He stopped for a red light and held her gaze. "I'm going to take you home. I'll call the house to update the team on our visit with Henry. Then Silvia can start working her magic."

The light changed and he pushed the car into motion, refocusing on the road, yet never losing the soft edge to his tone. "Take some time to shower, sleep, whatever you need to do to recharge, but they'll be on the case in the meantime."

"Where will you be?" Her heart rate quickened inexplicably.

"Watching your house from the street. I'll wait for you."

She opened her mouth to protest, but Kyle shook his head.

"No arguments. Plug your address into that GPS you love so much. And if you decide you want to stay with the team, you can pack a bag and we'll be on our way."

Humor and concern. A bubble of warmth burst inside Eileen.

Apparently the layers she'd sensed hidden behind Kyle's gruff exterior hadn't been so far-fetched after all.

EILEEN STOOD just inside her front door, gave Kyle a quick wave then shut the door.

She'd left no lights on earlier and darkness stretched through the interior like the sense of loss that had infiltrated every inch of her body.

Jack was gone. The reality of the past day was that simple.

As of this moment, she had no one. No one but Patrick and The Body Hunters.

What she wouldn't give to have the last five years back. All the time she could have been spending with Jack, she'd spent running from Robert's ghost.

What a fool she'd been.

She made her way through the house without turning on a light. After all, she knew every inch of the place by heart. Yes, she'd been gone for five years, but her renters hadn't touched a single piece of furniture other than to keep things spotless and fresh, waiting for her return.

Maybe that's what she'd do now, for Jack. She'd head over to his apartment tomorrow. Surely the police would be done by now and she could straighten up whatever sort of mess they'd made. She'd keep the plants watered and the mail sorted. She'd vacuum. She'd dust.

She'd keep everything ready for Jack's return. *If* he ever returned.

Shock gripped Eileen by the throat, wrenching a sound so foreign and raw from deep inside her she wasn't sure she'd made it.

Grief and loss, fear and disbelief, battled for position inside her, and she sank to her knees. She wrapped her arms around her waist and gave in to her emotions, gave in to her fears. She cried, letting the sobs wrack her body, letting her tears slide down her face, dripping from her chin until she could cry no more.

A noise sounded from out in the kitchen and she swallowed, dragging a hand across her damp face.

Eileen.

Had someone whispered her name?

Another noise.

A click—like the sound of her patio door sliding shut.

Footsteps sounded from the stone pavers out back and she launched herself into motion. Had someone been inside her home? Watching her? Going through her things?

She wrenched the kitchen phone from the wall at the same moment the dark silhouette out back caught her eye.

Her stomach caught and twisted, tipping sideways inside her.

"Jack?" she cried out. The height was right. The build.

The figure stilled, turning in her direction, kicking off the motion-sensitive floodlights she'd installed not long after she moved back home.

She pressed 911 in the same instant the light flooded the yard, bathing the intruder in white light. A dark ski mask covered his head and face, yet, in the split second before he turned and ran, the light caught the distinctive color of his eyes.

The sight left Eileen so breathless she could barely speak when the emergency dispatcher came on the line.

"State your emergency."

"There's been an intruder." Eileen forced the words through her tight throat.

There's been an intruder, she thought, *with my brother's eyes.*

"There's been an intruder," she repeated, this time spelling out her address in a state of numb disbelief.

For the intruder's eyes hadn't been Jack's.

They'd been Robert's.

Either he had a twin, or he'd chosen this particular moment to return from his watery grave.

She'd come home to face the ghost from which she'd run away.

Her own words bounced through her mind as she waited for the dispatcher's instructions. A cold dread gripped her, refusing to let go.

Either her mind was playing serious tricks, or the ghost she'd come home to face had decided to find her first.

CHAPTER FOUR

Body Clock: 31:15

K yle was in motion the moment the floodlight flashed to life in the space behind Eileen's foursquare.

He'd been waiting for her to turn on a light inside the house, when the sight of the still-dark house juxtaposed against the sudden bright light out back gave him reason enough to charge in, expecting the worst.

He was inches from the front door and closing in a dead run, when the carved wooden monstrosity eased open.

Eileen stood inside, still in the dark, her wide, scared eyes lit by the streetlamps behind Kyle.

"Which way did he go?" Kyle asked, taking one look at Eileen and knowing *someone* had put that look there.

"Took off out back."

Kyle moved to rush past her, but she gripped his

53

elbow. "He's gone."

"Are you sure?"

She hesitated momentarily then nodded. "Very. My yard opens into a small park connected to the street out back."

"Dangerous."

"Beautiful...on most days." She squeezed her eyes shut, visibly working to gather her wits. "I called it in."

"To the team?"

"To the police."

"Then we have to move quickly." He brushed a hand against the dark wall but didn't find what he wanted. "Where are the damned light switches?"

"Sorry," Eileen said softly. Her quick touch against the opposite wall bathed the hallway in a soft glow from an overhead fixture. "It takes a second to brighten."

Kyle hooked his fingers beneath her chin, studying her frightened expression. Her eyes were rimmed with red, damp eyelashes clinging one to the other. She'd been crying. No wonder she hadn't turned on any lights.

The emotions of the day had more than likely overcome her once she had a minute alone and she'd let herself cry, let herself feel. Then what?

"Are you hurt?"

Eileen shook her head, stepping free from Kyle's touch. "What happened?"

She pointed toward the dining room and the archway between there and the kitchen. "I was crying, and then I heard the back door click. I think he was watching me. I'm not sure."

"He?" Kyle's investigative mind snapped to attention, wrenching itself away from the thought of bundling the scared woman into his arms.

Sirens sounded outside, drawing closer, and he knew he had to move quickly. He wanted to scan the apartment with his own eyes before the police arrived.

"Where did you first see him?"

She pointed toward the kitchen. "I was in the dining room. When I moved toward the noise, I saw his silhouette out back."

"You keep saying his."

"He was tall, athletic build. Definitely male."

"Did he see you?"

She hesitated.

Kyle grasped her shoulders, studying her. What was she holding back?

Eileen pressed her lips together tightly then spoke. "He saw me after I called him Jack." Embarrassment flickered through her eyes and Kyle's heart twisted. She'd hoped her intruder had been her brother.

"He turned to look at me," she continued. "That's when the spotlight triggered." She looked away for a moment then refocused on Kyle, but something in her eyes had shifted. "That's when he took off over toward the next street."

She wasn't telling him the full story, but he wasn't going to push her. Not now. The scream of sirens drew closer and he pushed away from Eileen, turning on lights as he moved through the house, searching for anything obviously disturbed or missing. He found nothing.

Eileen left him to let in the authorities and a moment later they'd been separated for questioning, standard operating procedure to keep their stories fresh.

An hour later, the police were gone, declaring the entire incident nothing more than an interrupted burglary that could have had a far more serious ending.

The phone rang, and as Eileen spoke softly to whoever it was on the other end of the line, Kyle moved through her home one more time, letting instinct guide him, instead of forcing the search.

He passed through the kitchen, narrowing his eyes at Eileen to ask the unspoken question. Was she all right? She nodded in return, and Kyle moved past her, headed for her office.

There, he saw only tidiness and order, a space that wasn't used as much as it was admired. He couldn't say where that particular thought came from, but yet, he couldn't shake it. What was there in this room to be admired?

Eileen had furnished the room with simple Shaker pieces, but she'd filled the bookcase with framed photographs.

Kyle stepped closer. Frame after frame detailed what appeared to have been a happy childhood and life on a farm. Yet, the photo of the couple Kyle assumed to be her parents sat aside from the rest, separated as if someone had moved it.

Kyle reached for the frame, but quickly stopped himself.

Footfalls sounded behind him, but he didn't turn. Not yet. He needed to study the faces. Study the expressions.

The young couple beamed as they bundled three young children into their arms, bodies wrapped in snowsuits, hats and gloves. Five faces. All smiling. All happy. All alive.

He blinked.

Eileen had never mentioned any family other than her brothers. Had her parents died not long after this picture?

"My family." Her voice sounded from behind his shoulder.

"I don't see them in any pictures after this." He spoke the question as a statement, hoping to ease the pain of the old heartache he somehow knew his words would resurrect.

"We were headed out into the snow to play." Eileen reached for the frame, but Kyle turned to block her move. Her eyes narrowed almost imperceptively before she continued. "My parents were leaving for a weekend getaway, the first they'd taken in years. We never saw them again."

"Accident?" he asked, although sudden images assaulted him with lightning speed. Flashes of metal and bodies. Broken glass. Broken bodies. Shattered lives.

"Something went wrong with the car and they

went through a guardrail. Supposedly they died instantly."

Kyle gestured to the rest of the framed shots. "And these?"

Eileen pointed at the photos one by one. "Jack and Robert. Me. Patrick. My grandparents."

"Patrick?"

"O'Malley." She smiled. "That's who just called. He's the U.S. Attorney for this region, but I've known him since he was just a young lawyer starting out. He was a friend of my grandfather's."

U.S. Attorney's office. Her brothers?

She answered the question before Kyle could give it voice. "Both of my brothers wanted to be just like him. First Robert and then Jack. He was like the father we lost and they admired him, emulated him." She shrugged a bit. "Patrick and I..." Her voice trailed away. "We never fully connected."

"Yet he just called you."

"Someone called him about my break-in." She smiled, the slight move turning up the corners of her mouth.

Her understated beauty struck Kyle again, and his heart rate quickened. He forced himself to focus on her words and not her face.

"He's *very* protective of me. Of us. Of all of us. He never had a family of his own."

Her gaze moved past Kyle, landing again on the last photo taken of her family. "I see you like that one."

He turned to study the frame, not quite understanding her statement.

"I keep it over on my desk." She took a step toward the shelves. "I appreciate the repositioning, but I like to keep this one close."

Kyle snapped his hand over her wrist in the split second before her fingers made contact with the frame. "You didn't put this here?"

She frowned, pulling her hand away from his touch, rubbing her wrist. She shook her head. "I assumed you did."

He shook his head. "I found it here."

"The police?"

Another shake of his head. "They were looking for things out of place. I don't think they would have touched this, but we can't be sure."

Eileen's frown deepened, creasing the soft skin between her eyebrows.

"Do you have a small paper bag?"

One half hour later, they were on their way. Eileen's packed overnight bag sat on the backseat beside the photograph and frame Kyle had carefully wrapped in the paper bag. He'd wanted to preserve any prints the intruder might have left behind, if he, in fact, had been the person to move the object.

Kyle didn't think they'd get so lucky, but assuming otherwise might cost the investigation evidence, and right now, evidence was in short supply.

But he knew his team, knew their determination and their investigative skill. All they needed was one break.

Maybe, just maybe, this would be it.

THE PRODUCER hadn't counted on the woman coming home so soon. After all, shouldn't she be out searching for her brother?

He chuckled to himself, pulling off his mask and raking a hand through his hair before he climbed into the backseat of his car.

"Where to, sir?" his driver asked.

"Home."

Much as he could use a drink and some socializing, this wasn't the time, or the place. How long had it been since he'd been able to let loose in public.

He sighed inwardly. A long, long time.

He pulled down the mirror along the sidewall of the car and checked his reflection.

His vibrant eyes gazed back.

If the woman hadn't recognized him, it would be a miracle, but he'd never been short on miracles, had he? Perhaps his luck would hold.

Perhaps the damned floodlights had made it impossible for her to see his eyes, although he suspected the opposite to be true, based on the look of stunned wonderment that had passed across her face.

He'd screwed up by allowing himself to act on impulse tonight.

Jack Caldwell had proven to be completely uncooperative. None of the usual methods had broken the man, and so the Producer had come here.

To the sister's home.

Perhaps she had what he needed. If not, perhaps she'd lead him to it.

He'd visit her again, but next time he'd be more careful, much more careful.

And sooner or later, he'd get what he wanted.

He always got what he wanted.

No matter who had to pay the price in the process.

KYLE FINALLY settled into his room a bit after one o'clock in the morning. He hadn't had time to unpack upon the team's arrival, not that it mattered. Truth was, he never had much to unpack on any of The Body Hunters missions. He was a man of simplicity. A few changes of clothing, a toothbrush, a bar of soap. What else did he need?

He dipped his hand into the pocket of his jeans and extracted his pocket watch, the one thing he'd miss if he ever lost everything. His father had been given the watch by his father before him, and to Kyle it represented not only family, but also survival.

He unsnapped the gold circle and peered inside, not at the workings of the clock and the reminder of how late the time was, but rather at the small photo he'd cut to fit the opposite side of the watch.

Sally.

The one thing he'd lost that had meant everything. After her death, nothing else had mattered for a very long time. Matter of fact, nothing else mattered still.

Eileen Caldwell's face flashed through his mind in direct opposition to the thought, but he squelched the image, focusing on his late wife's sweet smile. She'd been as blond as Eileen was brunette, as soft-spoken as Eileen was confident.

Kyle had his first vision the day Sally died. A vision he'd ignored, thinking he was losing his mind. The scene had unfolded as clearly as if he'd been watching a movie. An armed robbery. Ski masks. A hostage. A single shot.

He'd said nothing to his wife, not wanting her to think of him as anything but the quiet, strong man who would always keep her safe.

How soundly he'd failed her.

The coroner had tried to console Kyle, explaining Sally had never felt a thing. The single shot had been effective at ending her life instantly, and altering Kyle's existence forever.

He'd thought perhaps the first vision would be his only vision, yet the opposite had been true. The first had been just that, the first of many. Much as he'd tried to ignore the signs and images that flashed through his mind, sometimes they provided information just when he needed it most. An idea. A direction. A guide.

Some might call it intuition. Kyle called it an unwanted pain in the ass.

The most vivid images came at night while he slept, and more often than not, he relived his first vision at least once a week.

Sally had been gone for eight years and yet his mind hadn't gotten the message that the vision no longer mattered. Or perhaps his mind still worked to punish him, still worked to keep the guilt fresh, to sharpen the sense of blame he'd carried all these years.

Could he have somehow saved her life if only he'd accepted the vision as something other than a sign of weakness?

Most nights, like tonight, he'd avoid sleep for as long as possible, until exhaustion overcame his will to stay awake.

He slipped his feet out of his boots and tugged the fabric of his jeans down his legs and over his feet. He traded in his traveling clothes for running gear and headed outside.

While he knew venturing out at night into unknown terrain was an invitation for an injury, he had sense enough to stick to the road, and he knew his body and mind needed the physical release only running could offer.

A few moments later he rested his palms against the trunk of a majestic fir while he concentrated on stretching each muscle, readying his body for the workout it was about to receive.

Yet his concentration wasn't at his usual level. Not tonight.

He found his attention drawn to the safe house, to the lines of log and mortar, to the lights still burning behind the old home's windows.

He stared at one window in particular. The bedroom where Eileen apparently hadn't found sleep, either, based on the shadow that moved back and forth across the window.

Back and forth.

Back and forth.

Perhaps her pacing calmed her nerves and quieted her fears about her brother's welfare.

An uncharacteristic urge to go to her welled up inside Kyle, but he tamped it down. The woman had enough to worry about. She didn't need the company of a socially inept man who couldn't quiet his own inner demons. How would he ever help soothe the very real external demons keeping Eileen awake?

And so he ran, long and hard, into the darkness of the Pennsylvania night.

He ran until his lungs burned and begged for relief. He ran until his runner's high filled him with the sense of invincibility—the sense that he could master anything thrown his way, including the recurring vision of Sally's robbery and the recurring dream about the faceless woman, lost and frightened, running for her life.

He ran until he couldn't run any farther, and then, for good measure, he ran some more.

As he approached the house, surprise hit him at the light still glowing from Eileen's window.

He moved into the house and up the stairs, hesitating as he moved past Eileen's bedroom door.

A sliver of light escaped into the dark hall from the crack beneath the door, broken in the middle by a shadow, suggesting Eileen stood just on the other side.

Waiting? For him?

"Kyle?"

The sound of his name on her lips restored every ounce of tension drained by the run. Kyle drew in a deep breath and hesitated before making his move.

He wanted more than anything to answer her, and yet he longed to retreat to the cover of his own room, to the familiar silence in which he'd stayed hidden for so many years.

Going against all logic and all sense of objectivity, he made his choice.

He reached for the door.

CHAPTER FIVE

Body Clock: 37:05

Eileen heard Kyle return from his run, the sound of his footsteps growing nearer on the stairs. It was amazing to her that a man so large could move with the grace she'd witnessed as he'd started his run.

She'd heard movement outside and had peeked through her window in time to see him look away. From where? Here?

Her insides tightened at the thought.

Now, more than an hour later, she sat waiting for his return, waiting for the chance to talk to him, to hear his deep, yet gentle voice one more time before she closed her eyes and tried to sleep.

As crazy as it sounded, she needed his reassurance everything would be all right, when typically she didn't need anyone's reassurance about anything. Tonight, however, she needed someone to tell her Jack would be found alive and well. She needed someone to tell her she'd survive this ordeal no matter what.

That someone was Kyle.

His footsteps slowed outside her door, and she pressed a palm to the heavy wooden panels. "Kyle?"

She spoke his name so softly she wondered if he'd hear her, much less answer. To her amazement, the doorknob turned a moment later. And there he stood, skin glowing, eyes bright from his run in the cool night air.

She swallowed, wanting nothing more than to launch herself into his arms, but the thought was crazy. Theirs wasn't that sort of relationship. He was here to help her as part of The Body Hunters team, nothing more.

Yet, without saying a word, Kyle stepped inside her room, his gaze never leaving Eileen's. He pushed the door shut behind him then reached for her hands, capturing her fingers inside his.

He smelled of heat and strength and she inhaled the musky scent, wishing she could tap some of the power he so obviously possessed to recharge her waning energy.

"How was your run?" She winced at the tentativeness in her voice, like that of a schoolgirl.

Kyle smiled, amusement dancing across his handsome features. "You waited an hour to ask me that?"

Heat arced between them, and Eileen couldn't deny what she felt. The attraction born on Isle de Cielo still survived, pulling her toward this man.

She shook her head.

"You'll be all right," Kyle said, as if he understood

her fears without being told.

"Am I that transparent?"

"No." He shook his head and held her hands more tightly. "You're human. Your brother's gone missing and a stranger broke into your home tonight. The logical question for anyone in your position would be whether everything will be all right again." He hooked his fingers beneath her chin. "It will."

But as much as Eileen wanted to believe him, she couldn't. She turned away from his touch, crossing to the window to stare out into the starlit sky.

"What happened that you're not telling me?"

Kyle asked the question, his voice sounding from just behind her, even though Eileen hadn't heard him take so much as a step. How could a man so big—so menacing—be so stealthy?

She turned, having to press back against the windowsill in order to avoid brushing Kyle's chest. "I don't know what you mean."

This time when he cupped her chin, his expression made it clear she wasn't to move away. "I think you do."

"I saw his eyes."

Kyle blinked, concern erasing any softness his gaze had held. "He was that close to you?"

Eileen nodded, flattered by his show of protectiveness. "When I called Jack's name, the man turned toward me. He kicked off the sensors, and the floodlights caught him full in the face before he ran."

"I thought you said he wore a mask."

She drew in a steadying breath, reliving the moment in her mind's eye. "He did, but the contrast of the dark mask only made his eyes more vivid. I only know one person with eyes like that."

Kyle's brows pulled together. "Jack?"

Eileen shook her head, laughing a little. "You're going to think I've lost my mind."

His fingers slid from her chin to her cheek, cradling her face. A knot of restraint deep inside Eileen broke, filling her with the courage to confide in Kyle.

"It was Robert."

Kyle tensed. "Are you sure?"

Defensiveness flooded through her. "You think I imagined it."

His expression tightened.

"I didn't," she continued without waiting for his answer, her voice threatening to break.

But then Kyle did something so unexpected, Eileen fell speechless.

He pulled her into his arms and held her. Simply held her.

After a few moments, he spoke softly into her ear, his lips brushing against her hair. "I know you didn't imagine it."

In his words, she heard the voice of a believer, the voice of someone who knew exactly what she meant.

Eileen pushed back far enough to study him, far enough to search the depths of his eyes for whatever it was he wasn't telling her.

The shutters on his emotions slid quickly back into place, as they always did, but not before she had a glimpse of the passion and caring the man so carefully guarded.

Kyle took her hand and led her to the bed, sitting down to pat the mattress beside him. "Together with the team we'll figure out what's going on. Searches and reports on the handwriting and prints are running downstairs even as we speak."

Along with the picture frame, Eileen had brought a handwritten note from Jack for comparison to the alleged suicide note. Martin and Silvia had jumped at the chance to analyze both.

Eileen sat down beside Kyle, aware of the heat between their bodies. "Thanks for believing me."

He nodded. "Try to rest. I'll stay until you fall asleep."

They stretched out side by side. Kyle draped his arm across her like an anchor—providing comfort yet also ensuring she went nowhere without him during the night.

Her every nerve ending crackled with the nearness of him, with his touch.

She thought of their time together on Cielo and of the afternoon she'd taken Kyle and Will to a sacred chapel along a rocky cliff. She'd twisted her ankle during the climb, going down hard.

Will had continued on, but Kyle had stayed with Eileen, holding her steady, his sure touch testing her ankle bones and ligaments for signs of serious injury.

She thought of those same hands now, wondering what it would be like to feel Kyle's touch again. What would it be like to make love with this man—a man who overwhelmed her just by being?

Heat flushed her face and she drew in a sharp breath.

"Are you all right?" Kyle rolled her toward him, searching her face with a guarded look.

Oh, how she longed to tap into the emotions he held so carefully in check.

"I will be." She nodded.

He pulled her closer, his moves those of a protector, nothing more. "Try to sleep." His gentle voice reached deep inside her and soothed the part of her that had shattered the moment Patrick had told her Jack was missing.

Eileen closed her eyes and pictured her brother's face and smile. She imagined his voice. And then she slept, filled with the dream everything would be all right somehow.

When the first light of morning eased through the room's windows, she rolled over to find Kyle gone. Yet no more than two hours earlier, she'd awakened to find him still beside her.

His breathing pattern had suggested he'd been awake, but Kyle hadn't moved, hadn't left her side. He'd stayed with her, guarding her from the unseen foe that had violated her family and her sense of security.

Eileen had said nothing. She'd settled back into Kyle's arms, letting his warm embrace ease her into the deepest sleep she'd had in days.

She smiled as she stripped out of her clothes from the night before and turned on the shower.

At that moment, she felt safe. She felt secure.

Kyle had stayed with her long after she'd fallen asleep. Even more importantly, he'd believed what she'd seen.

The comfort of those two things was enough to help Eileen brace herself for the challenges of the day ahead.

KYLE'S RUNNING SHOES pounded against dirt and rock as he veered from the road into the woods.

Had he lied to Eileen when he'd told her everything would be all right? How could he say such a thing when his world had never been the same again after he'd lost Sally?

He had no right to make promises he couldn't keep.

He kept his second run shorter than the first, pulling the crisp, dry air deep into his lungs. While he had to admit the cool air here provided an instant burst of energy, he missed the familiar dampness of home.

But a run was a run, and he'd needed this run badly.

The unwanted sexual tension and attraction he'd experienced holding Eileen in his arms had blindsided him.

While she'd slept, Kyle had lain awake, as he did every night. But last night's insomnia had far different roots than his usual sleeplessness.

Last night, his mind had worked and reworked one basic question. Would he give himself permission to get to know Eileen—to fully know her?

He admired the woman, of that there was no doubt. She was a woman of intellect and compassion, a woman who put the needs of others first. He'd seen those attributes in action firsthand during his time on Cielo. Yet, the glimpses of her life he'd witnessed since he'd arrived in Pittsburgh suggested she was a woman who had experienced more than her fair share of heartache.

Adding to the puzzle, he'd never heard her speak of a lover, either past or present. Had she isolated herself from the risk of emotional pain just as Kyle had? By choice?

No one would ever guess it to look at her. The effervescence she'd exuded on Cielo had understandably been missing during the past day. Her reserved presence and unspoken fears were indicative of the person she was at heart. A realist and a damaged soul.

And Kyle couldn't do a thing to squelch the pull he felt for her.

Part of him wanted to ease Eileen's pain, longed to wipe away her past and future heartaches with one swipe of his hand. But an even bigger part of Kyle knew that particular desire was nothing more than an uncharacteristically emotional dream.

Emotions had no place in an active investigation, and his certainly had no place here. Following the clues to the best of his ability did have a place, and was the way he could best serve Eileen.

The sooner the team found Jack, the sooner Eileen would find closure—one way or the other.

With that in mind, he pulled to a stop outside the safe house's kitchen door and stretched quickly. Then he stepped inside, grabbed a tall glass of water and headed for the case room.

With any luck at all the analyses run overnight would give the team something concrete to work with this morning.

As Kyle stepped into the room, Martin sat hunched in front of a computer screen, his focus glued to what appeared to be a continuous scroll of names and numbers.

Silvia sat next to another machine, yet busied herself with something completely foreign to databases and computer searches.

Her hands worked a needle and thread as she pieced together geometric cuts of cotton cloth. Sea-green. Royal-blue. Purple.

She'd started a new quilt, as she did with every new case.

"For Eileen's brother?" Kyle tipped his chin toward her work.

Silvia smiled without looking away from what she was doing. "I went with soothing colors."

"She'll like that."

Silvia looked up at him, took in his workout gear then frowned. "I thought I heard you go running last night after you and Eileen got back."

Her expression shifted from curious to mother-hen mode.

Kyle knew now was the time to steer the conversation away from his inability to sleep and back toward the case.

"Any luck overnight?" He pointed at the humming machines.

"Handwriting program zeroed in on some interesting differences." Martin's voice sounded from across the room.

"We're still hoping for a hit on the one print we lifted that wasn't Eileen's," Silvia added.

Martin had fingerprinted Eileen digitally upon their return last night. She'd matched all but one partial print taken from the frame.

Kyle replayed his conversation with Eileen in his mind, zeroing in on the one thing she'd been most hesitant to share. The uniqueness of her intruder's eyes.

He could find no logical explanation as to why Robert Caldwell would have chosen this moment to return from the land of the presumed dead, but what if he had?

"You're running criminal prints?" he asked.

Silvia and Martin both nodded.

"Noncriminal?"

Again, two nods. "We ran all of the departments included in the response call to her house."

"And?"

"Nothing." Martin shrugged.

"What about something a bit different?" Kyle asked.

Martin squinted. "Civil records?"

Kyle nodded as he spoke. "Just call it a hunch."

Silence beat between the three.

"How long would that take?" Kyle asked.

"A few hours, give or take a few."

Kyle grimaced. The body clock was ticking and a few hours were a few too many. "What if we narrowed the search a bit?"

"You have someone particular in mind?" Silvia asked.

This time it was Kyle who shrugged. "Try the Western Pennsylvania United States Attorney's office."

Martin's brows lifted. "Full staff?"

Kyle shook his head. "Attorneys only, but make sure you set your starting parameter back several years."

"Why don't you just give me the name?" Martin asked, curiosity shining in his eyes.

"What makes you think I have a name in mind?"

"Just call it a hunch," Martin said flatly.

Kyle knew when he was about to be cornered. Silvia had stopped her hand-stitching, and Martin had moved away from the computer screen.

The team had always abided by the need-to-know rule. Martin and Silvia didn't need to know what Eileen had seen. Not yet.

"Thanks," Kyle called out over his shoulder as he headed for the hall. "Briefing time?"

"Seven sharp," Silvia answered. "You've got fifteen minutes."

"I'll be back in ten."

With any luck at all, he'd be back in five. He wanted to be in that room when the fingerprint match hit. And his intuition, roaring back to life, told him that was exactly what was about to happen.

A SOFT KNOCK sounded on Eileen's door as she stepped into a pair of khaki slacks and a warm sweater. She slicked a brush through her wet hair and reached for the door.

Maggie Connor stood in the hall, holding two steaming mugs of coffee. "I thought you might like some company and some coffee."

Maggie's warm smile crinkled the skin at the corners of her pale eyes and Eileen nodded, moving aside to let her friend enter.

"How are you?" Maggie asked, concern apparent in her expression. "Did you get any sleep?"

Eileen opened her mouth to reply but instead answered only with a nod.

It didn't take a rocket scientist to realize Kyle was a private man—a man more than likely not commonly found comforting an agency client in the middle of the night.

She was sure he wouldn't be happy if the rest of the team knew about his late-night visit…and stay.

Eileen gestured for Maggie to take the room's lone chair.

Maggie's gaze narrowed and Eileen realized her friend had been looking for more than a nod.

Eileen thought about telling Maggie how she couldn't seem to get past the shock of Jack's disappearance, and about how she refused to believe history could repeat itself so cruelly.

She thought about describing the intruder's eyes, and how she couldn't shake the feeling she'd been staring at her long-lost brother Robert.

She thought about telling Maggie everything, and yet, she told her nothing.

Even though she knew she could trust Maggie, Eileen had so perfected the art of denying her own feelings she wasn't sure she knew how to share them. Not yet.

Maggie took a sip of her coffee and nodded toward Eileen. "You'd better drink up. Silvia and Martin have been up since before dawn and based on the chatter in that room, they've found something."

Hope blossomed deep inside Eileen's chest. Would today be the day the team would unravel the mystery of Jack's disappearance? Would they find him?

She drank a large gulp of hot coffee and headed for the bathroom. "I'll be ready in five minutes."

Maggie reached for her as she passed, gently touching her arm. "I know how scared you must be. And I want you to know we'll do whatever it takes to bring Jack home."

Her friend's kind words wedged a crack in Eileen's armor. A knot of emotion clogged her throat. "I know you will."

Moisture shimmered in Maggie's gaze. "Will and I would have never been able to bring Jordan home if it hadn't been for your help...and your friendship. Let us help you now."

To an outsider, the exchange might have seemed odd considering The Body Hunters were already onsite and hard at work, but Eileen understood the deeper meaning of Maggie's words.

As guarded as Kyle might be with his emotions, Eileen was the same—if not more so—and Maggie knew it. She'd sensed Eileen's pain and grief when they'd first met, just as she saw through her tough facade now.

"Deal?" Maggie asked, searching Eileen's face.

Eileen nodded, tears blurring her vision. "Deal."

Maggie gave her a quick hug then tipped her chin toward the bathroom. "Now, go dry that hair. Daylight's wasting and we've got a brother to bring home."

CHAPTER SIX

Body Clock: 42:00

J ust as Maggie had described, the case room buzzed with activity. Kyle and Martin stood huddled by one of three computer workstations, both men's features drawn tight in concentration.

They glanced in her direction, and Eileen nodded a greeting, doing her best to ignore the way her chest tightened when Kyle's eyes softened at the sight of her.

Will and Silvia stood deep in conversation at yet another workstation, so Eileen followed Maggie's lead and dropped into a chair. She couldn't help but notice the colorful scraps of material pushed to the side on the table in front of Silvia.

She warmed inside, recognizing the older woman's handiwork instantly. A quilt. For Jack.

Eileen flashed back on the quilt Silvia had lovingly and quickly made for Will and Maggie's daughter Jordan, never doubting the girl would be found alive.

To Eileen the scraps of material stood for Silvia's hope and the team's belief in their work. Like puzzle pieces of the mystery they'd taken on, the multicolored shapes would come together to form the whole —the result an indisputable work of art.

Eileen could only pray this particular body case would bring Jack home as smoothly as she knew the quilt would take shape.

"Eileen?" Will's voice shattered her thoughts. "Maybe you could help Silvia work this hotel system to our advantage."

Eileen stepped to Silvia's side, recognizing the program on the monitor instantly. She reached for a piece of paper and scribbled a list of function keys, then pointed one by one to the commands she'd made note of.

"These will let you set parameters for specific date ranges, search by client name, and sort by frequency and length of stay."

"What about cross-checking names?" Will asked, his gaze riveted to the screen.

"Unless you have a particular name in mind, that's going to take some good old-fashioned desk work."

He pursed his lips then locked stares with Eileen. "We found your older brother's stays."

She raised her brows.

"He seemed to favor quarterly three-day stays over a period of two years with a higher concentration of reservations during the fall he disappeared," Silvia explained.

"Why?" Eileen shook her head. "He lived in the city.

It doesn't make any sense."

"Part of a case?" Will asked.

Myriad thoughts whirled through Eileen's brain. "I can't imagine any other reason, but he never talked about it."

"Would he have told you?" The corners of Will's eyes softened.

"No," she answered honestly. Neither of her brothers shared information on cases in progress. They'd both learned to remain close-lipped, just like their mentor Patrick.

Yet based on what Henry the bartender had said, Jack had zeroed in on Robert's hotel stays. The question was why? And what had he found?

She leaned closer to the desktop system. "May I?"

Will nodded as he eased out of her way. She reached past Silvia and quickly entered two sets of dates from the list of Robert's stays. An alphabetized list of names flashed onto the screen.

"If we check this manually, we just might find a repeat of a second or third name. Then we can check those against the remaining dates." Eileen shrugged. "You never know. We might get lucky."

"Thanks." Will gave her a reassuring look. "In the meantime, let's go over what we do have. Martin?"

Eileen headed back to her seat, her attention captured by the whir of Silvia's printer pulling the names she'd just sorted.

The fact Robert's visits to the hotel had grown in frequency just prior to his disappearance suggested whatever it was he'd been involved with had escalated. Had he met with foul play as the result of an investigation?

And had Jack met with foul play because of his obsession with Robert's past activities?

One person would have a better feel for what had happened than anyone. Patrick O'Malley.

Martin projected a sampling of Jack's handwriting from both the alleged suicide note and the note Eileen had provided onto a large screen. He stood next to the images, pointing to the height of the letter strokes.

Eileen straightened, forcing herself to focus on the moment, the here and now. Today was about finding Jack and about proving he never wrote any damned suicide note.

"I had an analysis system compare the two samples for me overnight. What I found was that while the patterns of slant and size are similar, the length of the signature is different. Typically, this aspect of a person's handwriting doesn't vary.

"You're saying the suicide note is a forgery?" Kyle asked.

"I'm saying it could be." Martin's features tightened. "It also could be authentic. The writing lacks the starts and stops, the hesitation marks and uneven ink coverage you'd find in most forgeries. It's almost as if Jack wrote this under extreme pressure."

"Maybe someone held a gun to his head?" Eileen repeated the question she'd asked Patrick just yesterday.

Martin nodded. "Exactly." Then he drew in a deep

breath and pinned Eileen with a quizzical stare.

"What?"

"Does anyone in your family have similar handwriting to Jack's?" he asked. "Some blood relatives have almost identical writing styles."

She struggled to find her voice, thinking again of the intruder's vivid gaze. "Robert."

Martin squinted. "Deceased?" He dropped his voice as he spoke the word as if realizing too late the impact his question would have.

"Allegedly."

Kyle's rich voice filtered across the room from where he stood, features set as if in stone. Eileen gave him a sideways glance of gratitude. It had been a long time since anyone had referred to anything about Robert's disappearance as alleged, and she appreciated Kyle's kindness.

She pushed out of her seat and approached the photos of Robert and Jack tacked to the case chart. "Our grandparents used to tell us the boys were spitting images of our father when he was younger." She trailed a finger first across Robert's image, then Jack's. "But yes, they've always been very much like each other, right down to their handwriting."

"And you?" Martin asked.

Confusion twisted inside Eileen and she shook her head. "Me? I've never been anything like them."

"Your handwriting?" Martin pushed a blank sheet of paper across the table. "May I have a sample?"

Surprise slid through Eileen, but she did as he asked, bending to sign her name before she handed the paper back.

The young operative frowned down at the loops and curves of her signature and the spacing of her letters. "Completely different."

"Both of my brothers were left-handed…" Eileen caught her slip of the tongue. "*Are* left-handed. I'm not."

"Well, I'd say you have grounds to question the validity of this note." Martin swiveled back toward the computer. "And if your brother Jack *did* write this, I'd guess he didn't do so by choice."

"WHAT ABOUT THE photo frame?" Kyle pushed away from where he'd been leaning against the wall, pacing once across the room and back.

Silvia shifted toward the second workstation, taking over the briefing. She projected a series of partial fingerprints onto the screen. "We were able to lift several latent prints, as you know."

She advanced the image to the next screen, two clean prints taken from the set Eileen had given last night. Next to Eileen's prints, Silvia had manipulated the image to illuminate those partials that matched Eileen's.

"If you note the ridge patterns marked, you'll see that all but one latent belong to Eileen. Not a surprise."

She advanced the images again, and this time one partial print filled the screen.

"The owner of this print," she continued, "was a bit of a surprise. Because Eileen uses no outside help and

Kyle refrained from touching the frame, I worked on the assumption the print belonged to the intruder or a member of the team responding to Eileen's distress call."

She shook her head. "But we came up without a hit from either the criminal or law enforcement database."

Kyle fought the urge to drum his fingers against the wall. Had the woman gotten a match based on his suggestion to check the U.S. Attorney's office, or not?

He appreciated how much Silvia and Martin loved their work, and on any other case, chances were good Kyle would have enjoyed the detailed description of the matching process, but today he wanted the bottom line.

"And the match?" he asked.

Silvia smiled—a kind smile that suggested she knew exactly the route his thoughts had taken. "Too much information, my apologies." She held up a finger. "We did find a match in the IAFIS noncriminal database."

"IAFIS?" Eileen asked.

"Integrated Automated Fingerprint Identification System," Silvia explained. "Largest of its kind. Stores records for criminal and civil submissions."

"Who?" Eileen asked.

"A member of the United States Attorney's office here in Pittsburgh." Silvia tipped her chin in Kyle's direction. "We saved hours thanks to Kyle's hunch."

Circles of color fired in Eileen's cheeks. She shot a wary glance in Kyle's direction. Had she assumed he'd shared what she'd told him about her intruder in order to guide the search? Or was the flush of color in her cheeks due to the anticipation of having her suspicions confirmed?

But Silvia's next statement stunned not just Eileen, but also Kyle.

"Not just a United States Attorney's office employee," the older woman continued. "But the United States Attorney himself."

"Patrick O'Malley?" Will asked.

Silvia nodded and Eileen visibly sagged in her seat. Disappointment flashed across her face. The older man had no doubt been in her home countless times.

The team blew out a collective sigh. They'd found their match, but with it, had found no information of use.

"All right." Will held up a hand and moved to the front of the room. "The man's like an uncle to Eileen, so this shouldn't surprise us. It doesn't help us find our intruder, but we'll keep on moving. We don't believe in dead ends, remember?"

As Kyle watched, Eileen pulled herself taller in her chair and forced a tight smile.

The woman was a picture of practiced strength and calm, yet he couldn't help but wonder when that facade would crumble. He determined then and there to stick close.

If Eileen Caldwell's calm demeanor faltered, Kyle planned to be there to help her pick up the pieces.

Will clapped his hands together, capturing the attention of each team member. "Here's where we stand. The frame may not have helped our case, but we do have specific dates for Robert's stays at the Grand Pittsburgh Hotel. We also know Jack had become obsessed with information surrounding those stays, and we have reason to believe Jack may not have written his alleged suicide note. Next steps?"

But Eileen was already in motion, her determined strides headed for the door before Will had handed out assignments.

"Eileen?" Will called out.

"It's been a long time since I had Sunday brunch with Patrick." She spoke rapidly, as if she needed to act before she changed her mind. "Seems to me he can provide us with direction on every topic you just covered."

Will shot Kyle a look very clear in its meaning. After last night's break-in, Eileen was not to be left alone, nor was she to be given a chance to jeopardize their investigation.

Kyle stepped away from the wall and trailed Eileen toward her room.

She narrowed her gaze as she spun in his direction. "Are you following me?"

"Apparently so."

She dropped her voice so low he had to strain to hear her. "Did you tell them about Robert's eyes?"

Kyle shook his head. "I suggested where they should look if they wanted to save time."

"And they didn't question why?"

He smiled. "They know I don't like to answer questions."

Eileen opened her mouth as if she were about to attempt an argument, but then fell silent. She jerked a thumb toward her bedroom. "I need to freshen up a bit. Patrick is a man who only eats his Sunday brunch at the finest establishment in town."

"Is that an invitation for me to change my clothes?"

She tipped her head to one side, making a show of studying his jeans and denim shirt. "Only if you want to."

"No, thanks, then." He smiled.

She didn't try to hide her amusement. "I suppose this means you're going to ride along with me?"

"Is that another invitation?"

Eileen drew in a slow breath. "I suppose it is."

"In that case, I'll be right here waiting."

EILEEN WAS NO FOOL. Kyle had no intention of letting her get out of his sight. He also had no intention of letting her screw up the team's case.

She couldn't blame him. Her emotions raged inside her, a tangled mess of nerves and fear and hope and disbelief. It wouldn't take much to send her over the edge, and based on her tenuous relations with Patrick, attempting conversation with him when she was this keyed up might very well be the straw to break her control.

Eileen gripped the bathroom vanity and studied her reflection in the mirror.

Try as she might, she couldn't think of a single time she'd seen Patrick touch that frame since she'd returned from Cielo. Yes, she'd left her family photos behind in Pittsburgh, but they'd been tucked away.

She'd dusted them off and set them out within the past several weeks, and Patrick hadn't set foot inside her home or office until yesterday morning.

So how and when had his print ended up on that frame?

She thought again of the intruder's eyes, and a fresh wave of grief flashed through her.

Obviously, the man she'd seen hadn't been Robert.

The more she thought about the shadowy figure out back, the more she began to wonder whether she'd imagined the whole episode.

She'd been overwrought with sadness at the thought of losing Jack. Perhaps her mind had been playing tricks on her.

There had been no sign of forced entry. No theft of any kind. Nothing moved or disturbed.

It was her word against the evidence—or rather, lack of evidence.

She closed her eyes and rolled her neck. She'd so thoroughly convinced herself the man in her apartment might have been Robert she hadn't prepared herself for any other possibility.

In her mind she'd conjured up the likelihood of a conspiracy theory—something absurd yet plausible that would explain both Robert and Jack's disappearances.

A case they'd worked on. A conviction they'd made. Something—anything that would bring them home alive.

She splashed cold water on her face then set about

styling her hair and applying makeup. She might be drawing a blank on when Patrick had been inside her office, but she was sure there must be a logical explanation.

In the meantime, she and the team had questions. With any luck at all Patrick would have the answers they needed.

The man had never been forthcoming about the work of his office, but with Jack missing perhaps good old Patrick would change his ways.

Somehow she couldn't picture him being anything but the tight-lipped bureaucrat he'd always been.

She could hope for something different, yet her gut told her hoping was nothing but a colossal waste of time.

CHAPTER SEVEN

Body Clock: 44:05

A lmost forty-eight hours had passed since Jack made contact with his office, claiming he was taking the afternoon off to take a drive.

The ramifications of the passing hours reverberated in Eileen's brain as she stared out the passenger window, working and reworking the pieces of Jack's case as Kyle drove toward downtown Pittsburgh.

Will had promised to call as soon as the rest of the team sorted the hotel records, and Eileen and Kyle had promised to head straight back after their visit with Patrick.

What Eileen hadn't yet told Kyle was that she planned to request a second stop.

She needed to get inside Jack's house.

Will's source inside the police department had said the home hadn't yet been released from active investigation. The front door remained sealed.

Eileen supposed that was a good sign. If the police

had fully believed the suicide theory, the seal would be long gone.

In the meantime, she planned to get past the seal and inside. She just hadn't yet figured out how.

"Here we are again." Kyle pulled the car to the valet stand at the Grand Pittsburgh Hotel and cut the ignition.

"What can I say?" Eileen released her seat belt and reached for the door. "Apparently the Grand is the hotel of choice for the men in my family."

As she headed into the lobby to wait for Kyle, the sheer magnitude and beauty of the old hotel stole her breath away, as it always did.

An expansive marble staircase swept down through the center of the space. Tasteful groupings of ornate wing chairs and end tables warmed the lobby beneath the massive domed glass ceiling overhead.

How sad to think this beautiful hotel might have played a role in whatever it was that had happened not only to Jack, but also to Robert.

"Ready?" Kyle pressed a palm to the small of her back, his large hand firm against her spine, the move far more familiar than she'd been prepared for.

"Very." Eileen steeled herself as they climbed the stairs to the dining area above. She willed her mind to remain sharp and her tongue to remain under control once they found Patrick.

Kyle's palm never left her back, and she wondered how something so basic as the man's touch could infuse her with such strength.

Within moments of breaking Patrick's solitude and

joining him at his table, she realized both goals were lost causes. On a good day, the man's attitude tried her soul, and this apparently was *not* a good day.

Patrick's charcoal-gray suit and silver hair were flawless as usual, but something about his appearance seemed off. Lines of strain framed his eyes and mouth.

Had the reality of Jack's disappearance taken a toll? Had the mighty Patrick O'Malley's cool facade slipped?

Eileen kept the introductions brief, attributing Kyle's presence at her side as that of an old friend in town to provide moral support in her time of need. The explanation wasn't a total fabrication, but based on the sideways glance Patrick gave Kyle, the older man hadn't believed a word. Of course, suspicion was an integral part of his nature and his life.

"I'm glad you're here, actually. I've been worried about you." Patrick slid his focus from Kyle to Eileen. Something in his look stunned her momentarily. Genuine concern?

"Last night gave me quite a scare, but no harm done."

Patrick nodded, but said nothing more.

Eileen decided to forge ahead. "There's a photograph in my office. A photograph of Robert, Jack, and me with Mother and Father. Have you seen it?"

Patrick's eyes narrowed, but he remained silent.

"That framed photograph was the only item out of place after last night, and oddly enough your print was on the frame."

That got his attention. He sat back in his chair,

crossing his arms over his chest. "I wasn't aware the police took any evidence."

"They didn't." Eileen paused long enough to study the way Patrick glared at Kyle. Kyle, however, didn't so much as flinch. "Why would your print be on that frame?" she asked.

Patrick's expression shifted from annoyance to control, a move she'd witnessed countless times. "I admire that picture every time I'm in your home. Your mother and father and I were once quite close."

Eileen leaned forward, dropping her voice. "You haven't been in my home in years, and I can't seem to remember you leaving my sight while you were there yesterday."

Patrick tipped his head, adopting an innocent expression. "Well, I'm quite sure I did. You've had a shock, Eileen. You should be more focused on staying strong than on chasing phantoms."

Anger sliced through her. "You're talking about last night's intruder?"

Patrick leaned forward and took her hand. "The police found no sign of entry, forced or otherwise. Nothing was stolen. Nothing was misplaced." He squeezed her fingers. "They didn't find so much as a footprint out back."

Kyle cleared his throat. "If you're about to suggest Eileen imagined what she saw, you're going to find yourself outnumbered."

Patrick pulled away from Eileen, his full attention snapping to Kyle. "Young man, my family affairs are none of your business."

"Eileen's safety is my business."

Kyle spoke the words with such conviction both Patrick and Eileen fell silent, momentarily stunned.

"I witnessed the floodlight sensors being triggered myself, sir," Kyle continued. "Eileen didn't imagine a thing."

"Did you see this intruder with your own eyes?" Patrick asked Kyle. "Or did you merely see the light?"

"The light, sir."

"Then you really don't know what Eileen saw, do you? For all we know, she accidentally triggered the lights herself."

Kyle's glare grew lethal.

Patrick shifted his focus back to Eileen. "Are you as heavily medicated as your brother was?"

His question hit her like a slap to the face. "What are you talking about?"

"Jack was being treated for a serious clinical depression, did you know that?" He held up a hand before she could answer. "No, I suppose you didn't know, did you? You were out of the country and unavailable while Jack was grieving Robert's death."

Eileen knew Patrick hadn't approved of the years she'd spent in Cielo. This particular argument was not a new one.

Beside her, Kyle stirred, pressing his fist to his thigh. Eileen covered his hand with hers, out of Patrick's sight, and tightened her grip until Kyle relaxed his fist, opening his fingers beneath hers.

"His physician tells me his condition worsened six months ago," Patrick continued. "Just about the time he asked you to come home."

Eileen winced inwardly. Jack *had* asked her to come home. Many times. But she'd never dreamed he'd been in any sort of trouble.

"I came home," she said softly, her determined edge slipping.

Patrick sensed her weakness and struck an additional verbal blow. "Apparently a bit too late."

The impact of Patrick's words hit home, but it was his prior statement on which Eileen focused.

If Jack had been under treatment for a clinical depression, his physician should know whether or not he'd contemplated suicide.

"I want to speak to his doctor." Eileen straightened, renewed determination firing to life inside her.

"That won't be necessary." Patrick gestured for the waiter to bring his check. "The appropriate authorities are handling this investigation."

"You've already written Jack off as another suicide, haven't you?"

Anger blazed through Eileen like a brushfire, snapping her out of the numb disbelief that had dimmed her emotions and actions since she'd first received word Jack had gone missing.

"As difficult as this is for all of us, every indication points in that direction. Yes."

"And you're just going to sit back and believe that?"

Patrick said nothing.

"What about Jack's note?" Eileen leaned forward, fingers splayed against the expensive linen tablecloth. "Did anyone study the handwriting?"

Patrick nodded. "I personally had Jack's assistant verify the writing."

"Then Jack's assistant is wrong, because the writing doesn't match his usual form."

"And you know this how?" His tone grew skeptical.

"I do know my own brother's handwriting."

Patrick blew out a deep sigh, his countenance shifting to one of resignation. "You need to move past this, Eileen. Enough is enough. Leave the investigation to the professionals."

"So that's it?" Eileen rubbed her face, unable to believe her ears. "You're ready to write off Jack just like you wrote off Robert five years ago?"

Angry splotches of color marred Patrick's otherwise controlled expression. "I loved them both like sons."

"Did you?"

Eileen mentally chastised herself for her use of the past tense. Frustration simmered in Patrick's eyes. "Did I what?"

"Love them?" Eileen pushed to her feet, leaning across the table, not caring what the rest of the Sunday brunch crowd thought or heard. "Did you know Robert kept standing reservations at this hotel, and Jack had become obsessed with why? Were my brothers in danger? Did your office put them there?"

When Patrick spoke, he did so in a controlled manner, speaking slowly and purposefully. "Sometimes bad things happen to good people. Leave the questions to the professionals."

Eileen thought she might be reading into Patrick's

words until Kyle stiffened beside her.

Patrick had issued a warning, his delivery flawless.

Back off. Keep out of it. Mind your place.

Based on his body language and the set of his mouth, their discussion was over.

Eileen had always asked too many questions for Patrick's taste. And while he'd actively recruited Robert and Jack for the U.S. Attorney's office, he'd steered Eileen anywhere but.

Hell, he'd cheered the loudest when she'd been accepted into a hotel management program.

She'd always thought he'd wanted to keep her in a line of work considered risk-free, but maybe he just hadn't wanted to deal with her.

Was that why he'd favored Robert and Jack? Because they'd always believed whatever Patrick had said?

"I have a right to ask questions." Eileen met his shuttered gaze, her stare never wavering.

Impatience flashed in Patrick's eyes. "You never did understand the value of discretion."

Something deep inside Eileen snapped, and she flashed back on her childhood and the day Patrick had breezed into their lives seemingly out of nowhere.

She dropped her voice low. "How is it that you and Grandfather came to be such good friends? As best I can remember, you simply showed up one day wanting us to call you Uncle Patrick."

Patrick stilled and a bit of fire slipped from his eyes. "Enough, Eileen."

This time, she didn't stick around to argue further.

She left the table and Patrick O'Malley behind as she dashed for the exit, not caring whether Kyle followed.

Not caring about anything.

She'd been blinded by a sudden wave of grief and anger and years of missing her parents...her family.

"Whoa." Kyle grasped her arm and turned her toward him as she hit the lobby. "You all right?"

Tears blurred her vision, but she blinked them away. "He brings out the worst in me."

One brow lifted as Kyle spoke. "I think the feeling might be considered mutual." He tipped his chin toward the hotel exit, sliding his hand from her arm toward her back. "Let's get some air."

THEY WAITED for the car without saying another word. Kyle waited until he'd pulled away from the hotel before he spoke.

It had taken every ounce of self-control he possessed for him not to reach across the table and wring Patrick O'Malley's neck. But Kyle respected Eileen, and he knew she wouldn't have appreciated him interrupting the exchange she'd just shared with O'Malley.

Perhaps even more importantly, Kyle had an investigation to protect. Tipping off O'Malley to Kyle's true role might jeopardize The Body Hunters work. And so Kyle had bitten back his urge to interrogate the U.S. Attorney.

He wasn't about to hold back the questions he now had for Eileen, however.

"Do you treat all the father figures in your life like

that?"

Kyle wasn't sure what sort of answer he expected, but the sharp laugh Eileen let slip took him completely by surprise.

"Our grandfather took over our father's place, not Patrick."

He chose his next words carefully. "So the fact you two are at odds is strictly…"

"A battle of wills that started the day we buried my parents. He tried to step into a void that had already been filled by my grandparents."

She'd never offered details about her parents, other than to say they'd died in an accident.

"How old were you?" Kyle asked.

"Six."

Old enough to feel the pain of knowing your parents were never coming back. He winced. "I'm sorry."

Instead of waving away his kind words, Eileen took Kyle's hand in hers and squeezed. "Thank you. One moment we had a normal, happy family life and the next moment it was gone. Robert was the oldest. I think it changed him the most." She dropped her voice low. "But losing them changed us all."

Kyle realized they were more similar than he'd imagined, he and Eileen. They'd both lost loved ones and had lived with the scars ever since.

"Did the police ever determine why they lost control of the car?"

Kyle read Eileen's tense expression out of the corner of his eye. "No, and I never understood how it could have happened." She shook her head. "My father was so careful, so methodical. My brothers were—are —just like him in that way."

She swallowed visibly, shot Kyle a tight smile, then turned away to look out the window.

He let the moment pass, let the rest of his questions go unanswered.

He understood her heartache, understood how difficult the past was to revisit.

Sometimes silence was the kindest conversation of all.

Eileen reached for his arm, applying light pressure to his elbow, something akin to mischievousness dancing across her features. "I have an idea of how we can kill a little time."

Apparently silence wasn't what she had in mind after all.

Kyle lifted one brow in question, and Eileen didn't wait for him to say anything more.

"How good are you at getting around police seals?"

CHAPTER EIGHT

Body Clock: 45:40

T he neon-yellow police seal greeted Kyle and Eileen at Jack's front door.

Like Eileen's foursquare, Jack's home backed up to a neighborhood park, meaning one side of the house, as well as the back, had no adjoining structures.

Kyle frowned. "In case you hadn't guessed as much, midmorning is not the recommended time for breaking and entering."

He spoke the words under his breath as he took Eileen's arm, leading her around the side of the house.

He moved like a cat, a large, feral cat, sure of every step, no fears about what might be around the corner. He was a man completely in control, a man who could take care of himself, yet when he shot Eileen a tight smile, the look on his face could only be described as gentle.

How did he do it? How did he hide the caring side of

himself so effectively? Eileen had glimpsed enough to know the hard shell was just that—a shell. But what would it take to unleash the emotions kept so carefully guarded beneath the surface?

She walked beside him arm in arm as if she'd done so a hundred times. They followed the beautifully maintained brick path along the side of Jack's house, admired the garden of wildflowers her brother had loved since they'd been kids on the farm. Behind the house, they found a bistro table and chair, well cared for and painted a vibrant red.

"Doesn't look like the yard of a guy with depression issues to me." Kyle squeezed her hand.

The kind words and touch warmed her inside, bolstering her resolve to prove Patrick O'Malley wrong about Jack.

"Ready?"

Kyle's question signaled their shift into action, and Eileen nodded in answer.

He dropped her arm to study the back of the house, even as he approached the set of exterior French doors that led into Jack's kitchen. The home followed a similar design to that of Eileen's, and she couldn't help but wonder if this wasn't the exact manner in which her intruder had cased her home.

Kyle appeared to focus anywhere but the door, the move so effective Eileen wouldn't have noticed his hands working the door's lock if she hadn't been watching for it.

"Security system?" Kyle asked softly.

Security system? Eileen honestly didn't know. The

fact she knew little about Jack grew more apparent with each step of their investigation.

"I don't know."

Kyle pulled something so small from his inside jacket pocket his hand fully concealed whatever it was.

Eileen opened her mouth to comment, but the set of French doors had already swung open. A shrill squeal cut through the otherwise quiet setting and Kyle launched into motion, moving swiftly to silence the source of the noise.

He'd bypassed the system in less than five seconds. So much for security—not to mention how quickly he'd gotten inside without leaving a mark on the door.

Eileen trailed her hand along the edge of the door as she stepped inside then pushed the doors shut behind her.

"Where did you learn to do all of this?" Their gazes locked.

Kyle gave no answer, but the adrenaline and heat dancing in his dark eyes revealed another sliver of what made Kyle tick. He loved the thrill of the chase. The rush of the search.

For Kyle, every move he made served a single purpose: to bring the victim home.

As quickly as emotion had flashed through his eyes, the protective shield slid back into place. "Don't touch anything if you can help it unless you have a pair of gloves handy. I'd suggest we start in the bedroom or office."

And with that, Kyle moved out of sight.

Eileen stood motionless, like a smaller boat locked into place momentarily by a more powerful vessel's wake.

She realized then that her suspicions about Kyle had more than likely been correct all along. Had he lost someone who had meant the world to him? Did he carry an old wound, a scar on his heart that had shaped him into this fiercely determined warrior for justice? A man determined to save the world so long as he kept his own heart out of the line of fire?

She wanted to know Kyle inside out. She wanted to understand this man who picked locks, silenced security systems, and held her while she slept. All with equal ease.

A blinding need and desire rocked her to the core, leaving her unnerved and shaken.

Eileen looked up to find Kyle studying her, his expression a tangle of concern and impatience. "Are we doing this?"

KYLE WATCHED the emotions play out across Eileen's face—a combination of fatigue, determination and something he hadn't seen there before. An emotion he couldn't quite place.

He had to admire the woman's courage, her stubbornness.

She'd stood up to Patrick O'Malley like a champ this morning, questioning the man's arrogance and controlled responses when many a more powerful person would have simply stopped arguing.

"Are we doing this?" he repeated.

He knew from personal experience there was no easy way to face a loved one's belongings after that loved one was gone.

After Sally's death, his first response had been to toss every article of her clothing—every shoe, every purse, every trace of a reminder.

He'd been left with nothing but a broken heart. Many a sleepless night had passed in which he'd longed for one of her sweaters or scarves to inhale, hoping for a whiff of the perfume she'd loved.

Kyle forced his focus from the past. Some things were better left behind. He needed to focus on the here and now—on the body case at hand.

On Eileen.

She dragged a hand across the classic features of her face, and he wondered if the move was made out of pure exhaustion or to hide her emotions.

Until Eileen, he'd never met another person as guarded as himself. His heart gave an uncharacteristic pang of longing, but he shoved the sensation away, turning instead toward Jack Caldwell's living quarters.

"I'll meet you back there," he called out, torn between giving Eileen a moment to collect herself and his desire to gather her into his arms to promise he'd make her world of hurt go away somehow.

He pulled a thin pair of gloves from a pocket of his jeans and slipped them on, moving through the hallway, checking each doorway as he passed. When he hit the bathroom, Kyle stepped inside, reaching automatically for the medicine cabinet.

One shelf sat empty, perhaps marking where bottles of antidepressants had been found and taken into evidence.

He scanned the rest of the space, finding nothing else of interest.

He spun on one heel and slammed into Eileen, grasping her upper arms to catch her before he knocked her completely off balance.

She eyed his gloved hands and a smile tugged at the corners of her mouth. "Gloves? Any other tricks up your sleeves?"

He continued to hold her, pulling her a fraction of an inch closer, never taking his eyes from hers.

"Boy Scout," he answered, grinning ever so slightly.

His voice had gone husky and the shift in atmosphere wasn't lost on Eileen. Her gaze widened as she searched his face, her throat working.

A series of rapid images flashed through his mind. He and Eileen together, partially clothed, breathing hard—a blur of hands skimming across bare skin and bodies joining.

Heat blazed through Kyle and he dropped his hands from her arms, taking a sudden backward step.

Concern shimmered in Eileen's gaze as she reached for his arm. "Are you all right?"

He stared momentarily at the spot where her touch burned through the cloth of his shirt, and he nodded.

Then he moved past her, needing to put space between the two of them before he did something he might regret for a very long time.

He stepped into Jack Caldwell's office, taking a visual inventory, but finding nothing out of place. He opened each desk drawer methodically, but spotted no date book, no file folders, no personal data device.

"You've done this before?"

Eileen's voice broke his concentration.

"Searched a victim's home?" He gave a sharp nod and dipped his focus back to his work. "Yes."

Eileen moved beside him, placing her hand over his to stop his motion, to end his avoidance of her question, of her.

"You've searched a loved one's things?" She tilted her head as she asked the question, her expression conveying her realization she was about to cross a very personal line. "You've touched tangible reminders of who that person was?"

Kyle thought about lying, thought about filtering the truth. Instead, he decided to be truthful, but brief.

"I have." He did his best to ignore the moisture pooling along Eileen's lower lashes. "But that's not relevant today."

His curt response stung her. He watched her reaction, ached as she turned away, a protective veil lowering once again over the gaze that had just taken a tentative step toward breaking down the walls between them.

When she inhaled sharply, he reached for her, thinking she might be about to cry.

Instead, she reached for a small wooden box sitting next to the desk lamp.

Kyle thought about reminding her not to touch the

object, not to leave her prints, but instead he said nothing, sensing the importance of the box.

She visibly drew in a breath as she lifted the lid. Her shoulders sagged as she peered inside.

"It's empty."

"What is it?"

"I gave him a worry stone when he was in college. He promised me he'd always keep it with him. I wonder if he had it when he...went missing."

"There's one way to find out. What did it look like?"

"Its shape is nothing unusual, but its color is luminescent, like a star. I always told Jack to shoot for the moon and he'd land among the stars." Embarrassment colored her cheeks. "It's corny, I know."

Kyle shook his head. "No, it isn't. You two were once close?"

She nodded.

"Closer than you and Robert were?"

A shadow crossed Eileen's features and she nodded again. "Yes."

Kyle flipped open his phone and called Will, asking him to touch base with his police department contact to determine whether or not the stone had been found at the overlook.

Kyle knew the prospects of finding an oval stone at a rocky outcropping were slim to none, but he had to check...for Eileen's sake.

"I was about to call you," Will said after Kyle described the stone. "We have a match on the hotel records."

Kyle's pulse quickened. Perhaps they'd finally get

the lead they needed to move the case forward.

"Nicholas DiMauro," Will said slowly.

Kyle let out a low whistle.

DiMauro was one of the wealthiest men in the country—an international real estate developer with a gift for turning any project into gold.

"What do you think?" Kyle asked. "Informant or target?"

"Silvia's working on that now. How soon can you two head back?"

"We're on our way."

Kyle disconnected the call and reached for Eileen's hand. "Let's go. We're due for a debriefing."

And with any luck at all, this time the team would come away from their meeting with a better idea of what had happened to Jack Caldwell.

The body clock was ticking, and the passing time wasn't doing the team—or Jack Caldwell— any good.

JACK REGAINED consciousness slowly, his body protesting the repeated beatings he'd taken at the hands of his abductor's goon.

The Producer, his abductor had called himself.

Had the man completely lost his mind?

"I see you're ready for another round."

Jack rolled painfully to locate the source of the Producer's voice, only to spot him sitting in a folding chair, leaning forward, hands crossed over the handle of a baseball bat—a bat with which Jack had grown increasingly familiar during the past several hours.

"Are you ready to tell me where to locate what

I need?" the other man asked. "I've had your home searched and my men found nothing, nothing at all."

Jack worked to speak, the once simple action having become a bit like treading through molasses.

"Not stupid enough to keep them there."

His abductor stood, towering over Jack, dangling the bat from his fingers. "Then where?" His voice turned to a growl, his fury palpable.

"Under your nose once," Jack groaned. "You just didn't know it."

"Enough." The man called the Producer turned for the door, handing the bat to his lackey. "Don't stop until he passes out or talks, whichever comes first. And when he wakes up, start over again."

His abductor vanished through the doorway and the second man bounced the bat menacingly from one hand to the other.

As he stepped close, Jack could only hope his unconsciousness would be swift and long-lasting.

CHAPTER NINE

E ileen had gone quiet on the ride home and Kyle knew his actions were the reason for the distance.

He'd shut her out when she'd tried to reach him.

An unfamiliar sense of guilt nagged at him. Typically he wouldn't think twice about cutting off a client's too-personal questions, but this time was different.

This client was Eileen, and she deserved better.

The Body Hunters team had assembled in anticipation of Kyle and Eileen's return. Kyle briefed them on the meeting with Patrick O'Malley and their lack of findings at Jack's house.

He described the empty medicine cabinet shelf then asked what he saw as the obvious question. "Any ideas on how to find out the name of Jack's psychiatrist or the list of medications he was taking?"

Kyle directed the question at Silvia and Martin,

who did not disappoint.

The younger agent grinned as he handed him a sheet of paper. "Somehow I knew you were going to want that."

Kyle glanced down at the name and address printed on the sheet of paper. Walter Sanford. "How —"

"Insurance records. The United States Attorney's office offers top-notch medical coverage for their employees." Martin winked. "Did you know you can access just about any part of your medical history online if you know where to look?" The younger agent puffed up like a peacock. "I am good."

"And humble," Silvia teased.

"According to Jack Caldwell's history," Martin continued, "his last visit to Dr. Sanford's office was more than six months ago, and his records show no prescriptions as being filled and paid for during the past year."

"Doesn't mean he didn't pay cash to hide the paper trail," Kyle said.

"There is that," Martin conceded.

"I've already placed a call to Dr. Sanford's emergency number posing as Jack's concerned aunt." Silvia gave a quick shake of her head. "The dear doctor was less than cooperative. Insisted he hadn't seen Jack in months, so he had no idea of whether or not Jack had been having suicidal thoughts."

"Yet, the police found antidepressants." Eileen stated the fact on everyone's mind.

"Maybe they were planted there by someone," Silvia answered.

Silence filled the room as that possibility sank in.

"In the meantime," Silvia continued, "I've been digging into the life of Nicholas DiMauro."

She tapped a few keys on the desktop keyboard and a photograph appeared on one wall. "Meet Mr. DiMauro, as if any of you hasn't seen his photo everywhere recently."

DiMauro had recently bought up a huge section of the Las Vegas strip, declaring his intent to implode several massive casino complexes in order to return Vegas to the casinos and nightclubs of the strip's roots.

The move was nothing short of genius, if you calculated the amount of free publicity DiMauro's announcement had generated.

The image was like the man himself, larger than life. His perfectly coiffed hair in no way betrayed his age. Neither did his face, which was line-free and tanned the color of someone who spent more time on the golf course than in the boardroom, even though DiMauro was a self-professed workaholic.

"Among his varied interests," Silvia said as the projected image changed to one of DiMauro in a Pittsburgh Pirates ball cap, "is DiMauro's undying love for his hometown teams."

"Which would explain his frequent stays at the Grand?" Will's voice sounded from across the room.

"Potentially." Silvia tapped the keys once more and the next face to appear on-screen was none other than the head of the Basso crime family. Richie Basso.

"But it wouldn't explain why his dates of stay

matched Robert's or why the Basso family holds a thirty percent stake in DiMauro's Las Vegas project."

"You think Robert was investigating the DiMauro and Basso link as far back as five years ago?" Kyle asked.

Silvia nodded. "It's possible. And it would make sense for Jack Caldwell to have become obsessed by the pair's current relationship, considering his recent indictments."

It was Eileen who spoke next. "Then they were both playing with fire."

The focus of each team member shifted to Eileen. Each face was lined with concern and the knowledge their investigation went far deeper than faces on a wall for their client and friend.

"That's exactly what we're going to find out," Kyle said. He reached for Eileen's hand, not caring that the rest of the team saw the gesture.

She cast him a grateful but guarded smile.

"And your timing is impeccable," Silvia continued. "The Pirates have a home game today. Matter of fact, I'd imagine the stadium is starting the seventh inning stretch as we speak."

Martin pulled two Pirates caps from a bag. "You're going to need these, and our local contacts suggest waiting outside the Grand's back entrance for DiMauro's return from the ballpark."

Kyle blinked. The Body Hunters' varied resources never ceased to amaze him.

"You may also need these." Martin reached two more objects across the table to where Kyle and Eileen sat. Body Hunters communicators. One of a kind and unrivaled in their transmitting power.

Kyle tucked one tiny object into his ear and handed the other to Eileen. He pushed to his feet, but Martin shook his head.

"One more thing." Martin handed both Kyle and Eileen a pair of sunglasses and tapped the right hinge on each frame. "Video cameras. The image will transmit here." He pointed to one of the computer monitors as he aimed a second pair of glasses at Eileen. Her image appeared on the screen.

While the image was crystal clear, the video transmitted no sound.

"Sound?" Kyle asked.

Martin shook his head.

"If you use these, we'll do our best back here to operate from the transmitted image alone."

"What if it's not sunny?" Eileen asked.

"Tuck them into the neck of your shirt, right hinge out."

"Understood—"

Without warning, the recurring vision hit Kyle with a sudden vengeance.

The faceless woman ran—panicked, entangled in dense foliage, frightened, her pursuer closing fast.

"Kyle?"

Eileen's voice broke through the scene playing out in his mind, and he refocused on the meeting.

Even so, he had to admit the images left him unnerved.

He hadn't been prepared for the intensity of the visions, stronger than any he'd experienced previously.

Was this a sign of a growing madness? Or the sign of danger to come?

Either way, he'd have to work harder to maintain control, to keep his part of the body case focused and on track.

He pushed away from the table, video glasses in hand, headed for the stairs.

"I'll be waiting in the car."

Right now he needed space. He needed distance. He needed action.

As long as he kept moving, he could stay one step ahead of the vision, one step ahead of whatever it was his psyche was trying to tell him.

If he kept moving, he might be able to stay ahead of the team's faceless foe and put himself closer to finding Jack Caldwell.

He could only hope.

EILEEN HAD CHOSEN not to question Kyle's hasty departure from the case room, yet even now, as they stood outside the back entrance to the Grand Pittsburgh Hotel, the look that had momentarily crossed his eyes haunted her.

He'd looked startled. No, more than that. He'd look frightened, and fear wasn't an emotion of which she'd thought him capable.

They stood a good thirty yards apart, each feigning waiting for a ride or friend, when the tiny voice-activated communicator in her ear crackled to life.

"Here he comes." Kyle's voice rumbled low in her

ear and sent her insides into an unnerving tailspin. "Looks like he's got a super-box full of people in tow."

And so he did.

DiMauro approached on foot, something that took Eileen by surprise. Even more surprising was the identity of the man walking beside him, also wearing a Pirates cap, but dressed impeccably in a charcoal-gray suit.

Ferdinand King, a man Eileen knew from his humanitarian—and not-so-humanitarian—work in the Caribbean and in Europe. The team had used King during their Cielo investigation to access crucial information, and in the end, King's own nephew had turned out to be the kidnapper.

"Do you recognize King?" she said softly.

"Son of a bitch." Surprise rang blatant in Kyle's voice. "What in the hell is he doing here?"

Their plan had been to follow DiMauro inside and approach him outside the hotel's private elevators, but Eileen's urgent need for information won out over their planned approach.

The moment she stepped inside the hotel door, she called out. "Mr. DiMauro?"

The older man spun to face her, his bodyguards each placing a hand to their side, readying their weapons, no doubt.

"Might I have a word with you?"

King excused himself, disappearing out of sight. Eileen found herself wondering if the man who typically wore only white had shifted to wearing gray out of deference for fall fashion colors in America, or as the result of finally feeling the tarnish of his own trade—the human trade.

DiMauro cracked a slow smile. "I've been known to be a sucker for a beautiful woman in a Pirates cap on many an occasion, but have we met?"

He made no move to approach her, yet he also made no move to walk away or ignore her advances. If anything, he seemed amused by her boldness.

"I believe you knew my brother." Eileen took a tentative step toward the man.

He smiled the practiced smile of a man who had given many interviews in his time. "I'd prefer to know you."

With that, Kyle stepped to Eileen's side. DiMauro's charming expression slipped instantly.

"Is there somewhere we can talk, Mr. DiMauro?"

DiMauro's two bodyguards had stepped between them, yet DiMauro remained where he was, apparently intrigued by the situation. "What is this in reference to?"

"Robert Caldwell," Kyle said flatly.

DiMauro winced, yet quickly recovered. "I haven't spoken to Robert Caldwell in years."

"But you did know him?" Eileen asked, her heart pounding in her chest.

DiMauro nodded. "Casually, yes."

"How?" she asked.

The infamous developer merely shook his head. "I'm not at liberty to say."

"Did you two meet in this hotel? Is that why your dates of stay overlap on numerous occasions leading up to my brother's disappearance?"

Her pulse quickened in anticipation of his answer. Was this how Jack had felt pursuing the connection between Robert and DiMauro?

DiMauro's response ended any hope she'd felt.

"I'm sure my dates of stay, as you call them, intersect with those of many others. This is the city of my birth, and as such, I visit whenever I can." He tapped his fingers to the peak of his ball cap. "Especially when the Pirates are in town. Matter of fact, I haven't missed a home game in years."

Eileen tipped her chin toward the bank of elevators. "I couldn't help but notice your companion. Ferdinand King?"

"Mr. King and I are old acquaintances."

"Another Pirates fan?" Kyle asked.

DiMauro smiled. "Precisely."

"What about your business dealings with Richie Basso?"

One of DiMauro's dark brows lifted. "I've never met the man but I understand he's made substantial investments in my newest venture."

Disbelief edged through Eileen. Kyle asked the question bouncing through her brain before she could open her mouth.

"He's financing thirty percent of your project, Mr. DiMauro. Do you honestly expect us to believe you've never met the man?"

DiMauro's expression darkened, any last remaining traces of charm vanishing. "What you believe is none of my concern." He snapped his fingers and his entourage launched themselves into motion. "This conversation is over. I have plans for the evening, and I've never been a man who keeps others waiting. Good night."

With that, he was gone, leaving Kyle and Eileen in his wake.

"What do you think?" she asked, turning to Kyle for a read on his expression.

Anger smoldered in his dark eyes and his mouth tightened, straining his handsome features. "We hit a nerve, and he definitely knew your brother. The question is how and whether or not whatever Robert was involved with led to foul play."

"And Jack?"

"If he started asking the same questions Robert had asked, there's no telling what might have happened." He grasped her hand and led her through the foyer toward the main lobby. "Let's see what your friend Henry has to say."

But when they arrived at the door to the bar, a young female bartender stood behind the bar, serving drinks.

They wound their way through the crowd of happy baseball fans, stepping as close to the bar as possible. Kyle lifted a hand to capture the bartender's attention. The young woman's warm smile slipped a bit as she realized Eileen stood by Kyle's side.

"Can I get you something?"

"Only a bit of information, if you don't mind." Kyle leaned forward and dropped his voice. "Can you tell me whether or not Henry will be on duty later tonight?"

The woman shook her head, sending her brunette ponytail swinging. "You know, he hasn't missed a weekend shift for as long as I've known him, but he had some sort of emergency. Can I give him a message for you?"

"No, thanks." Kyle shook his head and tossed a five-dollar bill onto the bar. "You have a good night."

"Now what?" Eileen asked as they climbed into the car a few moments later.

"Now we regroup."

And as they headed back toward the countryside outside Pittsburgh and the safe house, Eileen stared at the fading light outside the car.

Jack had been gone for over forty-eight hours. She knew enough to know they'd passed the critical mark in their investigation.

With every passing hour, their chances of finding him alive grew slimmer and slimmer. A shiver of dread raced through her.

She could only pray they'd find him before his time —the "body clock" as the team called it— ran out. If it hadn't already.

THE PRODUCER waited until the tramcar at the Monongahela Incline slid into motion before he made a move.

His quarry had met him as requested, and as expected, no one else rode the tram this late at night... this close to the midnight hour.

The lights of the city shimmered from across the

river, and the moon hung high and luminous in the sky.

When he finally spoke, the Producer did so slowly. "We meet again."

"Long time, no see." Henry smiled the confident smile that had always set the Producer's teeth on edge. It was the same smile that had made him such a successful bartender...and informant.

The Producer paced to the other side of the small tramcar, running a hand across the top of the wooden bench seat. "I understand your memory and your mouth both seem to be working overtime."

This time when their eyes met, the hotel bartender's smile held a bit less confidence and a bit more trepidation. "I don't know what you're talking about."

"Sure you do." The Producer reached behind his back for his gun. The compact object sat heavy and warm in his fist. "You've spent a lot of time recently talking to one of your regulars, Jack Caldwell." He raised a brow in question. "I can't imagine you're about to deny that. Not when I have eyes all over this city."

Henry didn't answer the question, he'd become too engrossed in staring down the barrel of the Producer's gun.

"Not so chatty now, are you?"

The Producer laughed, something he hadn't done much of in recent days.

Henry paled. "You have me confused with someone else."

The Producer shook his head, curving his mouth into a knowing grin. "I don't confuse easily."

The tramcar approached the station at the top of the incline and the Producer opened the car's exit door. He gestured with the gun from Henry to the door.

"That fall will kill me." Henry's eyes had gone huge.

"Now that—" the Producer tipped his chin and smiled "—is something on which we agree."

But Henry didn't move.

"It's either the fall or the gun. Take your pick." The Producer gave a dramatic shrug. "Fall from a tramcar? Bullet between the eyes? If I were a betting man, I'd say your choice is an obvious one."

When all was said and done, the loose-lipped bartender chose the fall.

Based on the way his body hit the wooded incline below, his days of mixing drinks were over. The Producer settled onto the unforgiving wooden bench for the return ride to the station below, and stared at the skyline. He wondered how soon it would be before someone stumbled upon Henry's body.

Then he realized the timing didn't matter.

No one would suspect anything other than a suicide jump.

After all, suicide jumps seemed to be quite popular this week.

CHAPTER TEN

Body Clock: 59:45

K yle glanced at his pocket watch and groaned inwardly. Almost midnight.

The team had entered day three of Jack's disappearance and still they were getting nowhere.

For the first time in as long as he could remember, Kyle needed something other than a run to ease the tension searing every inch of his soul.

He needed Eileen.

She'd remained distant on the ride back to the house, and he'd missed her easy chatter and her questions.

Perhaps the time had come to apologize for the way he'd acted back at Jack's house.

The house had fallen silent, an unusual event for The Body Hunters. Typically during a case, the safe house hummed with activity at all hours of the night and day, but tonight, the team rested and waited.

They waited and they thought. Each team member

no doubt wracking their brain for some piece of the puzzle they'd overlooked or incorrectly analyzed.

Kyle had heard Eileen moving around in her room. What was she doing? Pacing?

When he heard footfalls in the hall, he stepped outside his room, spotting the sliver of light beneath the bathroom door. The sound of rushing water followed.

Perhaps she'd decided a long, hot bath would soothe her battered spirit enough to help her sleep.

As for Kyle, there wasn't a thing in the world to ease his insomnia. So he waited, and he watched. Standing outside his bedroom door like a sentry, invisible and uninvited.

As if of their own will, his footsteps led him toward the bathroom. Toward Eileen.

Kyle hadn't been with anyone since Sally. He'd denied his body, denied his heart, and he'd succeeded.

Until now.

He leaned his forehead against the heavy wooden door and listened to her soft movements in the bath.

He should turn and walk away. He should sleep, just as the rest of the team was sleeping. He should go for a run.

He should do anything—anything but stand here, risking a surrender to temptation.

If he crossed the line with Eileen, he'd lose his objectivity on the case. He'd risk his focus, his effectiveness—both things she needed from him, for closure and for Jack.

Kyle listened for the sound of Eileen stepping out of the tub. Once he knew she was headed for bed, he'd walk away. He'd put the distance between them that needed to be there, for the sake of the case.

Yet, the sound that came from inside the bathroom was far different from what he'd expected.

Eileen let loose a soft sob, followed by another, and another.

"Eileen?" He spoke her name so gently he wondered briefly if he'd imagined his own voice.

But the sound of water splashing and the slide of the old-fashioned dead bolt being disarmed signaled he'd not only spoken aloud, but loudly enough for Eileen to hear him above her own tears.

She stood wrapped in a robe, looking up at Kyle, her hair twisted into a knot at the base of her neck, damp trails glistening on her cheeks, heartache blatant in her eyes. Kyle knew he'd lost the battle between emotional distance and the pull Eileen had over him the moment their eyes met.

He lowered his mouth to hers, brushing his lips lightly against hers.

She gasped, the sound startled, but slight, and he stepped into the bathroom, pushing the door shut behind him and sliding the lock back into place.

He sat on a hand-painted bench that stood against the wall and pulled her onto his lap. He cradled her against his chest and gently stroked her back.

"What was her name?"

Eileen's question startled him, the words worlds away from anything he'd expected her to say.

"How did you know?"

"Women's intuition."

Intuition. There was a topic he could live without discussing.

"Sally." Kyle hadn't spoken his wife's name aloud in more years than he could remember.

"You loved her?"

His heart twisted with the familiar hollow ache he'd worked to ignore since the day he'd lost Sally forever.

Kyle nodded. "Very much."

"How long were you married?" She touched her fingers to the back of his hand lightly.

Heat simmered between them where their bodies met, yet the heat was unlike anything Kyle had experienced. Theirs was not the heat of lust or carnal need. Theirs was born of the promise of recovery—the slow reawakening of two souls thought long dead.

"I never said we were married." He traced a finger across the back of Eileen's hand, amazed at the softness of her slender fingers beneath his bulky touch.

She drew in a sharp breath before she spoke. She'd felt the same thing he'd felt. At some point during the past two days, they'd connected at a level beyond Kyle's comprehension.

Eileen turned over her hand, capturing Kyle's fingers in hers. "You're not the sort of man to love someone and not do something about it. You're a long-term kind of guy. A marrying kind of guy."

Was he? He'd never thought of himself that way before, but perhaps Eileen was right. Perhaps he'd never loved again because he wasn't capable of doing so without the long-term commitment. Perhaps he'd just never met the right person.

But perhaps he was no longer capable of the emotion, the trust, the caring necessary to make love work.

He'd failed Sally at the most fundamental level a man could fail a woman.

Who was to say he wouldn't make the same mistake again?

A single image flashed through his mind's eye. The faceless woman, this time screaming. One word. Kyle's name.

He felt his skin go clammy as he shoved the image away.

Was the woman Eileen? Sally? Someone he had yet to meet?

"Kyle?" Eileen squeezed his hand. "Are you all right?"

And then he told her what he'd never told anyone else.

"I see things sometimes," he said slowly, feeling each word as he spoke it.

"Visions?" Eileen asked, her voice absent of any trace of skepticism.

How did she do it? In her presence he felt safe, when he was the one here to protect her.

Kyle nodded.

"You're intuitive."

He tipped his chin to study her, finding nothing but kindness and concern waiting for him in her dark eyes. "How did you know?"

She smiled, the move softening her already gentle

features. "I see in you a man who knows things, a man who feels things, a man who's sometimes scared to death of both."

Kyle swallowed down the knot in his throat, torn between continuing the conversation and leaving the bathroom while he had the chance, before Eileen could see any more deeply into the man he really was.

"I think we're all afraid of something," she continued. "I'm afraid of just about everything. I've run away my whole life. Why do you think I was in Cielo for all those years?"

Kyle shook his head.

"I couldn't face the fact Robert was gone, that he might be dead. I ran away. And I left Jack alone to shoulder the emotional burden." She lowered her head, staring down at their joined hands, dropping her voice to barely more than a whisper. "I'm a coward, Kyle."

He squeezed her hand and leaned to catch her gaze. "You're anything but."

She laughed softly. "You haven't seen me in action."

"I've seen all I need to see to know you're one of the strongest people I've ever met."

She drew in a deep breath and nodded her thanks, falling silent.

They sat like that for a long time, each with secrets newly revealed, shared between two people who had once been strangers but who now had become something far more.

"Do you have a picture of her?" Eileen asked softly.

Kyle reached into his pocket and pulled out the

pocket watch, handing it to her. She cradled it in her palm, then pulled her fingers free of Kyle's to gently open the treasured object, to study Sally's image.

"Oh, Kyle. She's beautiful." Her voice had gone tight with emotion. When she lifted her focus to Kyle's face, moisture pooled in her eyes. "I'm so sorry."

He nodded. "It's been eight years. Eight years since she died. Eight years since I had my first vision."

Eileen reached for him, tenderly cradling his face in one hand. "Whatever happened isn't your fault. It's not possible."

"I could have told her about the vision. I could have stopped her."

"Perhaps it wouldn't have made a difference."

"Perhaps it would have."

Suddenly, Kyle couldn't take any more sharing. He shifted Eileen from his lap to the bench then pushed to his feet, holding out his hand to her.

He stayed in her bed again, intending to leave as soon as she fell asleep, but unable to leave her side, her warmth.

Later that night, as Eileen slept and Kyle fought to keep his demons at bay, he realized he and Eileen had shared a connection more intimate than any physical coupling they could have experienced had they simply made love.

They'd joined on an emotional level, two lost souls reaching out to each other. Two guarded hearts cracking open the door to the possibility of more.

And as sheer exhaustion pushed against the edges of his conscious thought, Kyle did something he hadn't done in years.

He slept, his slumber dreamless, visionless and deep.

CHAPTER ELEVEN

Body Clock: 65:30

"You and I need to have a conversation."

The old anger and hurt simmered to life deep inside Eileen's belly as she took Patrick O'Malley's call the next morning. Kyle had left her room before dawn, and she'd already showered and dressed in anticipation of the day ahead.

"Correct me if I'm wrong, but we've already had our conversation."

"Not this one. I'll expect you here within the hour."

She glanced at her watch, annoyance battling curiosity. Six-thirty. What could the man possibly want at this hour?

"Where's here?"

"Exactly where you think it is."

The line clicked dead in Eileen's ear.

She knew where *here* was. Where Patrick had been

ever since he'd been appointed the United States At-torney for Western Pennsylvania—his corner office downtown.

She scribbled a note for the team, telling them only that she'd be back later. Guilt teased at the back of her brain as she sneaked into the hall and down the stairs undetected.

She and Kyle had shared so much last night, he'd be surprised by her disappearance today. Or would he? Perhaps the man's confessions last night had merely been good for his soul. Perhaps they had nothing to do with him trusting her, being attracted to her.

Her gut caught and twisted in direct opposition to her thoughts.

She shoved aside her doubt and questions and fo-cused on seeing Patrick.

Perhaps today would be the day she'd get the break she needed. Perhaps Patrick held the key to finding Jack and he'd finally decided to let her into the closed-door world of the U.S. Attorney's office.

She cranked on her car's ignition and pulled away from the house, driving slowly down the dirt path away from the safe house and back toward the city.

Kyle's image flashed again through her mind and she knew he'd be furious that she'd gone to see Patrick without him, but she wanted to make this trip alone. No, she *needed* to make this trip alone.

And with any luck at all, she'd be back before a sin-gle team member—Kyle included—noticed she was missing.

A short while later, Eileen sat across from Patrick,

his massive desk spreading between them, making his position of power and authority as clear as if he'd posted a sign declaring him boss.

"I'm only going to say this once." Patrick's expression took on an intensity she'd never before witnessed in his features. "Your little investigation—and I use the term loosely—has infringed upon an operation this office has been running for years.

"You will cease and desist. Now."

He slammed his fist down onto the desktop with such force Eileen found herself afraid of the man. The thought had never crossed her mind before.

Yes, she and Patrick had often found themselves at odds, but she'd never felt fear in his presence. Was her overactive imagination playing tricks on her? Or was her gut giving her a warning?

She refocused on Patrick's command, her mind locking on the one thing she and the team had done that might have caused such ire.

"DiMauro?" she asked.

Patrick's features tightened. "I'm not going to answer that question, nor will I comment on anything you might have to say. You may go now."

Anger simmered in Eileen's belly. "Not so fast. I am through being dismissed by you."

But Patrick merely sharpened his gaze.

Eileen decided to cut through the tap dance and get right to the meat of what she guessed was bothering the man. "I understand DiMauro's in tight with the Basso crime family. But then you probably know all about that, right?"

Angry color stained Patrick's cheeks, but he held firm to his silence.

Eileen made a show of pursing her lips. "Investments in his multibillion dollar Vegas project, I believe. I'd have to assume that's who you're going after. Is that what got my brothers abducted? Killed?"

Patrick's eyes narrowed. "Watch your step, young lady."

The remark made Eileen's blood boil, and she pushed to her feet. "That's where you're wrong. I am no longer a young lady you can order about. I'm a woman. A woman with my own mind, and if my mind says pursue Jack's disappearance like there's no tomorrow, then damn it, that's what I intend to do."

"And when you get in over your head and need someone to save your hide, don't come crawling to me." Patrick spoke the words through gritted teeth.

"Have I ever?"

He merely lifted one brow.

Eileen turned for the door, but not before she delivered her parting shot.

"How about Ferdinand King? He paid a visit to DiMauro last night. Is that part of your operation? Or are you going to tell me the man traveled to Pittsburgh just because the Pirates were in town?"

Eileen had one hand on the door when Patrick spoke, his words cutting her to the bone.

"In King's world, women and children are forced into lives not of their own choosing every day, but here...?" He stood and rounded his desk, gesturing to the window and the city outside. "Here an atrocity like human trafficking seems impossible, yet networks exist closer to home than you might ever expect. You have no idea of what danger you're flirting with."

He closed the gap between them, stopping mere inches from where Eileen held her ground. "You've hidden from reality for so long you have no idea what reality is."

"I know at least one of my brothers is out there somewhere in need of my help and you are not going to keep me from going after him."

She pulled open the door, working to remain calm as she stepped into his outer office. Her heart pounded in her ears and her mouth had gone dry.

Human trafficking? Was Patrick issuing a clue? Or a threat?

She steeled herself, letting the man's mightier-than-thou attitude slide off her back.

There was a time in her past when she'd tried to respect Patrick and his opinions, but something told her the time to stop had arrived.

She put one foot in front of the other, walking out of the man's office, her head held high, knowing that for once in her life, she was doing exactly what a responsible woman would do.

She was looking for her brother, and she intended to keep looking until she brought him home.

If Patrick or anyone else tried to get in her way, they'd better brace themselves, because she wasn't about to swerve left or right to avoid a collision. No. She intended to plow straight through anyone and anything that got between her and the family she loved.

EILEEN DROVE to the Majestic Overlook alone, wanting to be by herself with her thoughts for a while. She needed to stand in the place where both of her brothers had vanished. Had they died here? Taken their last breaths here?

She climbed from her car and walked toward the concrete outcropping designed to allow visitors the pleasure of experiencing the wonder of the rushing creek below.

She'd often laughed at the fact the swift current was called a creek. In her book, the Majestic was nothing less than a river—a force of nature to be revered and respected.

Eileen had never liked stepping to the edge, not even before her life had been turned upside down, not once, but twice, by fate and this place...and the faceless person or persons who had done *something* to her brothers.

She could feel it—the shock and disbelief of her loved ones as they faced their fate—just as clearly as she could feel the cool, autumn air against her skin.

She stepped toward the black wrought-iron railing, close enough to brush the tips of her fingers to the cold metal, but no closer. She pulled back her hand as if she'd been burned. Then she turned away.

She had no desire to see the rocks or rushing water below. She had no need to hear the oohs and aahs of the tourists with their cameras hanging from their necks. She desired only one thing...make that two things.

She needed to know what had happened here. She needed to know where her brothers were. Not just Jack, but Robert as well. She hadn't been ready to fight for her older brother five years earlier. Well, she was ready now.

Eileen was intelligent enough to know that shock and grief could play tricks on the mind. She knew the eyes she'd seen gleaming from her intruder's face were most likely not Robert's. But the man had spoken to her, hadn't he? Or had her mind conjured up the voice as well as the image?

She forced her mind from the question of what she'd seen to the question of what had happened in Jack's life to precipitate his disappearance.

What had her younger brother uncovered that had driven him to the edge of an obsession coworkers said left him a shell of the person he'd been before?

Eileen turned back toward the overlook, this time drawn by the sound of the rushing water below. She stepped toward the concrete outcropping, moving closer to the edge, closer to the railing that stopped waist-high. Had Robert or Jack or both taken their own lives here?

No.

She realized she'd spoken aloud when a family of four near her moved away, casting wary glances back over their shoulders.

No.

Neither brother would have jumped. It wasn't possible.

Had Jack encountered the same thing that had brought on the shift in Robert in the weeks before he'd vanished?

Had DiMauro played a role in whatever it was her brothers had gone through?

If the man thought Eileen believed he spent so much time in Pittsburgh simply to watch baseball, he must think her an idiot.

And she was far from an idiot.

Resolve filtered through her. Strength of conviction. An unflinching desire to see her family mystery to its end.

She stepped to the edge and looked over, ignoring the fear of heights that wrapped its icy fingers around her neck and squeezed.

She stared down into the rushing water, letting the sound wash over her. Letting her mind clear. Letting the thoughts and fears and doubts and questions wash away.

And then she turned back toward her car, needing suddenly to be with the team—to be with Kyle.

She raced toward her car, veering off the paved pedestrian path to save time, watching her step, careful of loose rocks from the overlook.

When she saw the stone, she took several steps before realization sank in.

Oval and luminescent, the small stone lay among the dirt and rocks.

She backtracked, dropping to her knees and fumbling for the small object. She plucked the stone from the ground and palmed it, her pulse rocketing.

Jack's worry stone.

Had he left it here by choice? By chance? As a clue?

She traced one finger lightly over the stone and remembered the day she found it and where—on their family farm.

The old farmhouse and barn had once been happy childhood symbols, but after her parents' deaths, the home she and her brothers shared had become an odd place. Strangers had come and gone, moving in and out of their lives as though emotions and bonds were fluid, never permanent.

Only Patrick had stayed, and for Eileen, he'd never been a source of much comfort.

Suddenly, she understood why she'd always run away from the difficult things in life.

No one had ever showed her how to stay.

And she realized something else.

Eileen knew exactly what she needed to do next—and where she needed to go.

She raced to her car and dropped into the driver's seat, reaching for her cell phone. When the other party answered, she spoke without greeting. "I need your help."

Several seconds later she disconnected, tossed the phone onto the passenger seat and cranked the ignition.

The time had come to face her past, whether she wanted to or not.

THE PRODUCER watched Eileen Caldwell from a distance, oddly conflicted by his desire to comfort the woman. Her emotional strain played out across her pretty features as she walked toward the edge of the overlook and back again.

Turmoil raged inside her, visible to anyone who could see.

Her family had been through more heartache and loss than most, and as the Producer watched the autumn breeze lift her shoulder-length hair and toss it about, he wondered if she felt alone.

He imagined she felt very alone.

Or maybe that was conjecture on his part. After all, she had lived on a Caribbean island for the past several years. Perhaps she liked being alone.

Her expression suggested otherwise.

The tense set of her mouth and the sadness around her eyes suggested she felt emotional pain. Loss. Uncertainty.

The Producer couldn't help but smile. He'd hoped for nothing more. He'd counted on nothing less.

Soon, she'd be ready to pay the price. Ready to do as he asked.

She moved again, this time stepping so close to the edge one well-placed push would send her toppling onto the rocky passage below.

He shuddered at the thought, uncharacteristically disturbed. He had no intention of pushing her to her death. Not yet.

There were too many witnesses here today.

He chuckled a bit to himself then sank down into his seat as the woman turned away from the railing and headed toward her car, walking briskly.

But then she stopped abruptly and dropped to her knees. She reached for something, but what?

Had his crew missed something of Jack Caldwell's? Had they left something other than the equipment he'd instructed them to trash and leave behind?

Eileen Caldwell pocketed whatever she'd found and hustled toward her car. The expression on her face turned the Producer's blood cold.

He knew that particular expression. He'd seen it on her face before. Years earlier.

Raw determination and fearlessness.

Rumor had it she'd lost much of her edge during the recent past, but the set of her features now hinted at a fire in her belly burning strong and bright.

She slid into her car, made a quick call then barely gave the ignition time to start before she peeled out of the lot.

The Producer knew exactly what he had to do.

As much as he'd wanted to spend more time with Jack, spend more time playing with the broken man's mind, he was faced with a new direction.

A new choice...or rather, a lack of choice.

Eileen Caldwell had stumbled upon something, and the Producer had to know what that something was.

So he did one of the things he did best, one of the things made easy by his secret persona and anonymity.

He turned the key in his car's ignition and pulled away from the overlook. Then the Producer followed

Eileen Caldwell.

The woman had stepped front and center on his radar screen and there was no shaking her now, not until he'd properly dealt with her.

Permanently.

CHAPTER TWELVE

Body Clock: 68:15

Kyle paced like a caged lion, a sense of foreboding wound so tightly inside him he thought he'd explode at any moment. Based on the expressions on the other Body Hunters' faces, he wasn't alone in his turmoil.

Eileen had vanished, leaving only a note that said she'd be back soon. Even worse, she'd left behind her Body Hunters communicator and video sunglasses. If she'd done something to put herself in harm's way, she'd have no way to reach the team except for a phone call.

Kyle had learned firsthand on many occasions that phone calls weren't what anyone would call practical during a time of crisis.

"She'll call. She probably needed to run an errand." Throughout the time since they'd found Eileen's note, Maggie had been the one person to try to soothe Kyle. She'd failed miserably. The rest of the team had known better than to try.

Silvia had placed a call to Patrick O'Malley, who had assured the older woman Eileen had been to see him that morning, but that she'd left hours earlier.

So where had she gone?

If ever Kyle's so-called intuition wanted to do something worthwhile, this would be the time.

Kyle's cell phone rang and he flipped the receiver open without checking the source of the incoming call.

"I need your help." Eileen's voice filtered across the line strong and confident.

Her voice sent a flood of relief rushing through him. He'd feared the worst when he'd noticed her absence and had found her note.

"Where are you?" He spoke the words flatly, successfully hiding the mixture of anger and relief sliding through his system.

"Headed to the farmhouse."

An image of a red painted barn and majestic home, once immaculate, but now in a state of disrepair, flashed through his mind's eye.

"My family's farmhouse," she continued. "Can you meet me there?"

Kyle grunted out his "yes" and Eileen rattled off the address. Kyle repeated it out loud, allowing Martin to input the information into the team's system.

"I found Jack's worry stone."

Kyle's every nerve ending came to attention. "Where?"

"The overlook."

He bit back a curse. She'd gone to the overlook alone.

"And?"

"And I thought about the fact I first found it at the farm. Maybe he dropped it to send me a message. Maybe whatever it is I need to find to locate him is at the farm."

He'd witnessed the phenomena on many occasions before during body hunts. The victim's family became expert at formulating convoluted explanations and theories.

Apparently the toll of the hours passed had begun to have the same effect on Eileen, but a trip to the farm might help. Who knew what evidence the team might uncover by looking at the victim's past?

"Kyle? You still there."

"We'll be there as quickly as we can."

By the time Kyle ended the call, the entire team was on their feet and in motion.

"Silvia, you stay behind to monitor our transmissions," Will said as he gathered equipment. "The rest of us will go with Kyle. Maybe today will bring our first solid lead."

"We can be there in forty-five minutes if we cut cross-country," Martin said, handing out maps.

Maggie squeezed Kyle's arm and smiled up at him as she headed for the stairs. Her thoughts might as well have been spoken aloud. She'd read the play of emotions on his face during the brief phone call. More than likely everyone had.

Trepidation tangled with relief. As much as he'd

tried to tell himself otherwise, Kyle was only human. While he wasn't proud of himself, he had to admit he'd given in to the emotional pull Eileen held over him.

He'd let her under his skin and into his heart. The sooner he admitted it, the sooner he could deal with it.

And as he and the rest of the team raced toward their fleet of vehicles, he wasn't sure what was more unnerving—the fact Eileen had gone off somewhere on her own when chances were very good their questions had drawn unwanted attention, or the fact his every ounce of focus had shifted from bringing Jack home to keeping Eileen safe.

KYLE FOUND EILEEN inside the stone farmhouse, flipping sheets off of old furniture. Dirt and dust clung to her sweater and jeans, yet her eyes were bright with anticipation.

"No one's lived here since my grandfather died seven years ago," she explained as the team filtered into the house. "My brother Robert tried to live here. The home was left to him, but he couldn't stomach the isolation. He missed the city and moved back within a matter of weeks."

"When was the last time you were here?" Will asked.

A look of shame crossed Eileen's face. "Seven years. Not since Grandfather's funeral."

"Not even after Robert vanished?" Maggie asked.

Eileen thinned her lips and shook her head. "I left

the country after Robert vanished. The last place I wanted to be was here—" she gestured to the sweeping ceiling and the plaster walls "—with the family ghosts."

"And Jack?" Kyle asked.

"Jack loved this place. I think he was devastated when Grandfather's will gave sole ownership to Robert."

"So you think Jack's been here?" Will asked.

"I know he's been here." Eileen widened her gaze expectantly. "Wild horses couldn't keep him away."

"What are we looking for?" Martin spoke up for the first time since their arrival. The youngest operative hadn't been in the field on previous cases and excitement shimmered in his gaze.

"Anything Jack might have hidden here. There had to be a reason he'd become so obsessed with Robert recently, and Jack was a stickler for documentation." She stepped toward the center hallway. "His notes have to be somewhere. And I'm only sorry I hadn't thought of this house sooner."

"Rooms?" Will's brows pulled together, his features tense with concentration.

"Kitchen, dining room, sitting room on this level." Eileen pointed toward the stairs. "Bedrooms, bath, and attic above." Another gesture, this one toward the far end of the hall. "Storm cellar and basement down that way."

"Fair enough." Will nodded. "Maggie and I will work the basement level. Martin, you work the kitchen and living areas. Kyle and Eileen, you take the top floors and attic."

"We're looking for books, journals, notes, file folders, boxes in closets, under beds, anything that might be useful," Kyle said as he moved to Eileen's side.

After the rest of the team had scattered, he reached for her arm and turned her to face him. "What were you thinking?"

She answered without questioning his meaning. "Patrick called and said he and I needed to have a conversation. I went to his office, had my head taken off for messing with one of his operations, then I drove to the overlook. I found Jack's stone, called you and drove here."

A chill slid down Kyle's spine. She had no idea of how many different security rules she'd violated by putting herself out in the open.

"You and I need to come to an understanding." Kyle pulled her tightly to him, his stare never leaving her surprised eyes. "From now on you don't make a move without me. We have no idea of what we're dealing with, but chances are pretty good we've pissed someone off by now. There's no reason for you to be going anywhere alone. Understood?"

She nodded, her expression solemn. "I didn't think."

Kyle broke contact, taking a backward step. "I need to run out to the car for something, but when I come back, you and I are going to rip apart the upstairs and you're going to tell me everything that went down today. Step by step."

He waited until she climbed the staircase before he slipped outside, heading straight for Eileen's car. As he'd hoped, she'd left it unlocked.

He opened the passenger door long enough to plant his GPS unit where she wouldn't easily spot the tiny instrument.

If she got the notion to go off on her own again, he'd be able to track her every movement.

In less than two minutes, Kyle was back inside the house, upstairs and listening to Eileen's story. She related everything that had happened that morning, and by the time she'd finished, guilt nagged at Kyle.

She'd done well, coming away from her meeting with Patrick with the strong suspicion DiMauro was involved somehow in a U.S. Attorney's operation.

Finding the stone had led her here and restored the light of determination to her eyes. He couldn't fault her for that.

"We're getting close, Kyle. I can feel it."

Something unfamiliar danced in her beautiful eyes, and Kyle recognized the emotion for what it was—something he hadn't seen there since they'd reconnected here in Pittsburgh.

Hope.

Any frustration or annoyance he'd felt with her when he'd found her missing disappeared then and there.

He slid his fingers down her soft cheek and smiled. "Then what are we waiting for?"

KYLE'S PROTECTIVE reaction to Eileen's early morning meeting left her feeling humbled…and safe. She couldn't remember the last time someone had cared whether or not she'd taken off unannounced.

She mentally chided herself. That wasn't entirely true. Jack had been upset with her on countless occasions over the years, especially after Robert had gone missing and she'd fled the country.

But he was her brother. He was supposed to care.

The fact Kyle was so worked up warmed her insides in unexpected ways.

She thought again of the intimacy they'd shared the night before, the kiss so tender she found herself questioning whether or not the brush of their lips had been real.

Was she falling for Kyle? If she were honest with herself, she'd have to say yes, but then, she'd never been fully honest with herself. Perhaps it was time to start. Perhaps it was time to put down roots and let someone into her life.

Reality squelched the idea as soon as it crossed her mind.

Kyle lived and worked in Seattle, and he was a man of habit. His wife was buried there, and Eileen was smart enough to know a man as set in his ways as Kyle would never leave the West Coast for the east except for the occasional Body Hunters case.

She'd be foolish to think he might relocate for her. And if Jack was found alive—which he would be— could Eileen bring herself to ever leave her brother again?

She found herself staring out a dirty and smudged

window instead of searching for Jack's notes. She forced herself to shut her mind to any wonderings other than those that might bring Jack home.

As the rest of the team worked throughout the home that had been in her family for generations, Eileen started her own process, taking each bedroom one at a time. Closets. Shelves. Under beds. In drawers. Behind furniture. Even behind radiators.

She found nothing except personal items and a few articles of clothing left behind by Robert and other family members through the years. Framed photographs. Dishes packed as if someone had planned to give them away or store them in the attic.

Nothing meant a thing, until Kyle returned from his search of the attic.

"This room is too small."

His statement shattered Eileen's train of thought and she shot him a frown. "What on earth do you mean by that?"

"It's not big enough. The attic above this part of the house extends for at least another three feet." He tapped on the wall, tilting his head to listen. "There's another space on the opposite side of the wall."

"A hidden closet?" Her mood brightened.

Kyle nodded. "Could be."

"When I was little—" she moved next to him, running her fingertips across the old wood "—rumor had it my ancestors ran liquor during Prohibition."

"I hardly think you'd store moonshine in a bedroom wall."

Kyle traced his palm over a crack in the wall and

stilled.

"No." Eileen had moved to the opposite end of the wall, keeping an eye on Kyle in case he'd made a discovery. "But maybe they kept records or something up here."

Kyle eased the hatch from the wall, exposing a second space, this one filled with archive boxes neatly labeled and left in a tidy row.

Eileen moved behind him, leaning to peer over his shoulder into the space.

The smell of aged paper assaulted them both. "Or something."

He reached into the tight space, sliding the boxes through the opening until not less than six boxes sat lined up, each marked with a starting and ending date.

Kyle shouted out to the rest of the team, and Eileen began the slow process of carefully removing each lid to peer inside.

Piles of loose papers, notes, photographs and journals filled each.

Yet one box stood out from the rest. One box had been organized, its contents rubber-banded into piles, handwritten notes detailing the contents of each stack.

Eileen recognized the handwriting instantly. Jack's.

"Jack did this," she said as Will, Maggie, and Martin moved behind her, looking over her shoulder to see what she and Kyle had found.

Eileen carefully opened what appeared to be an

antique, leather-bound journal. She flipped through its entries, each one nothing more than a date with a number and a list of physical descriptions—hair color, height, weight.

What on earth? Eileen's mind reeled. What had Jack stumbled upon and thought so important he'd organized and hidden the box and its contents?

"Who's B.C.?" Maggie asked, pointing over Eileen's shoulder at the tiny notation found at the bottom of each journal entry.

Eileen's heart ached as she touched a finger to one set of initials. "My mother. Betty Caldwell. These must have belonged to her, but what are they?"

Kyle sorted a stack of photographs, his coloring off, paler than normal.

Eileen reached for his arm. "What is it?"

Then her gaze fell to the subject of the photographs. Young women, in varying stages of dress, sat bound and shackled in a small, dark room.

One man appeared in the background of several shots. He appeared young and tall, but Eileen couldn't place him, and none of the shots afforded a clear view of his face.

She studied the journal in her hands one more time, realizing she held the documentation of horrors that had taken place at the farm.

"A kidnapping ring?" Kyle asked, handing the stack of photos back to Will.

Will flipped through each shot, blowing out a deep sigh and nodding as he handed them back.

"If there's a tie to DiMauro, this could explain why

you saw him in the company of Ferdinand King."

Kyle swore softly beneath his breath and Eileen fought to remain calm when all she wanted to do was run from the house and the box of horrors and never come back.

Martin had swung into analysis mode, studying the dates on each box and on every stack Jack had organized inside.

He nodded as he pointed to one notation. "Seems to be the last entry made by your mother."

His words drained the strength from Eileen and she sank onto her heels. Kyle reached for her, and Maggie dropped to her knees beside her just as Will's cell phone rang.

Will excused himself while Eileen read the note Martin handed her, working to wrap her brain around what she'd just seen.

"My parents died the next day. In an accident."

"Maybe it wasn't an accident," Martin said, drawing a sharp glare from both Kyle and Maggie. But the youngest member of the team didn't let their non-verbal warning slow him down any. "I'm just saying, maybe your mother didn't have a thing to do with all of this. Maybe she found a way to document what was happening. Maybe someone found out and had her killed."

Footsteps sounded in the hallway and Will rounded the corner, intensity blazing in his eyes.

"What is it?" Maggie pushed to her feet.

"We need to get back to the safe house." The set of Will's mouth had gone grim and he spoke without emotion. "Pack up everything and we'll process it there."

Kyle narrowed his gaze, asking the obvious question without giving it voice.

"They've found Henry the bartender," Will continued.

"Is he all right?" Eileen's voice sounded small and tired, even to her own ears.

"No." Will shook his head then called out as he turned away, "He's not."

THE PRODUCER sat in his car, far out of sight along a side road that ran through the Caldwell property.

He hoisted the binoculars to his eyes and waited, never taking his focus from the farmhouse and the line of cars.

Eileen Caldwell had assembled quite a crew.

Either she was quite smart, or not so smart at all.

If she found what he thought she might have found, her world would never be the same.

Under your nose once. Jack Caldwell's words haunted the Producer. *You just didn't know it.*

If Eileen Caldwell and her team had found what the Producer so desperately needed, he'd have to tighten the timeline he'd planned for her. There would be no time for smooth transitions. No time for niceties or civility.

He'd have to go in heavy and heartless. Not surprisingly, the thought of taking that approach instead of a more gentle one didn't bother him in the least.

The Producer had never been a man who favored

gentle.

He'd take heartless any day.

The small group emerged from the farmhouse, the three men each carrying large boxes and returning for more.

The Producer swore and smashed his fist down onto the dashboard.

Two things had just become apparently clear.

The Producer no longer had much use for keeping Jack Caldwell alive.

And he apparently now had a reason to want Eileen Caldwell dead.

CHAPTER THIRTEEN

Body Clock: 72:05

"We've hit a nerve with someone," Will said as he paced across the front of the case room, moving side to side. "Without knowing who that is, it isn't safe for Eileen to be anywhere but here."

"But you said Henry fell from the tram." Confusion tumbled through Eileen. "We don't even know if his death is related to Jack's disappearance."

"He worked for Jack."

Will's words hit her like a slap. "What?"

"He was one of your brother's informants. Apparently he wasn't too good about keeping his mouth shut and that may have gotten him killed."

Eileen thought about her recent conversations with Henry, the way he volunteered information about Jack, about Robert, about hotel patrons. Had her questions played a role in an innocent man's death?

Bile churned at the back of her throat but she bit back the sensation, instead sending up a silent prayer for Henry and whatever loved ones the man had left behind.

"How do you know your information is accurate?" Kyle directed the question at Will, who bristled ever so slightly at his friend's tone.

"The police and Patrick O'Malley have confirmed Henry's role. His death is being treated as a homicide."

"And Jack's disappearance?" Eileen pulled herself taller in her chair. Surely the authorities would look past their suicide theory now that Jack's informant had died under suspicious circumstances.

"I've been told the case is still open," Will responded. "Whether or not there's a connection between the two remains to be seen, but for our purposes, we'll act as though we now have two crimes instead of one."

He took a step toward the line of boxes waiting to be processed, and shifted his focus to Eileen once more. "And who knows what role your family actually played in those photographs we saw. But with both of your brothers gone, you're the last remaining family member in circulation. We need to face the fact our unseen foe may see you as his biggest threat."

Eileen squinted, her pulse quickening. "Me?"

Will pointed to the boxes. "Whether you like it or

not, you were there on the farm when all of this happened. You're a witness."

Beside Eileen, Kyle visibly tensed.

"I'm having a difficult time accepting any of this as true," Eileen said truthfully.

Silvia shot her a sympathetic look before she tapped on the keyboard, pulling a large map covered in notations up onto the projection screen.

The older woman began to talk, but Eileen's attention had been captured by Jack's quilt, which was coming together into a work of hope and color, soothing even in its unfinished state.

Eileen could only hope her younger brother would still be alive to receive and cherish Silvia's gift.

"And so you see," Silvia was saying, "the issue of human trafficking is a very real problem in all parts of the country, but the land and underground storage facilities once used during Prohibition do make things interesting around here."

Prohibition.

Eileen's stomach fell to her toes.

"According to family legend, my ancestors ran an illegal distribution network during Prohibition." She spoke the words flatly, emotionally detaching herself from their implication.

If her family had the underground facilities in place to store and distribute illegal liquor, what would have kept them from trading up from booze to women in an effort to get rich?

What seemed like hours later, the team continued to work diligently through the maze of boxes and documentation. They'd turned up nothing new, nothing but evidence of old crimes.

Then Eileen's hand stilled, her fingers tracing a recent notation in a new journal, this one apparently made in Jack's handwriting.

In his notes, he detailed a meeting with a Michael Downum in which Downum had provided proof of more recent kidnappings.

According to the notations, Jack had met with Downum months earlier, at about the same time cited by Jack's coworkers as the shift in Jack's personality and focus.

She handed the notes to Kyle, waiting to speak until he'd had time to skim the entry. When he'd finished, he lifted his eyes to her and frowned.

"Another informant?" Eileen asked.

Kyle tucked the notebook into his pocket, pressed his lips into a tight line and pushed to his feet. "Only one way to find out."

THE PRODUCER stood over the lifeless form of Jack Caldwell and pushed at the hostage's ribs with his toe.

"Did you kill him?"

Anger simmered inside the Producer as he glared at his man. Without Caldwell, the Producer had no pull to draw in the sister, Eileen. He supposed he could lie and say Jack Caldwell was still alive even if he wasn't. After all, it wasn't as though the Producer had never lied.

Hell, his entire life was a lie. A beautifully orchestrated, masterfully crafted lie.

"He's not dead, sir. I just pushed him like you told me to."

"And how did that work out? Did he say anything?"

The other man shook his head, fear shining in his otherwise vacant eyes, and the Producer laughed.

Of course Caldwell hadn't said anything. He was too stubborn. The whole damned Caldwell family was too stubborn, and the Producer should know.

He squatted next to Jack Caldwell and studied the slow rise and fall of his chest.

So the Producer's man wasn't a total idiot after all. Caldwell was still alive. Good.

For now.

He leaned close to Caldwell's ear, talking slowly and clearly, hoping that somewhere deep inside the man's brain there remained intellect enough to understand exactly what the Producer was about to say.

"If you think I'm going to kill you, Jack, you're right. But I'm going to let you live a little longer. Long enough to bring your precious sister to you. Once she gives me what I need, I'll let you two spend some quality time together.

"Forever."

When Jack Caldwell moaned, the Producer smiled.

Message sent and received.

THEY FOLLOWED Jack's notes to a small diner on the south side of the city. A pretty young blonde, no more than twenty-six or twenty-seven, worked the hostess desk. Her long hair had been swept into a loose knot at the base of her neck, and her full lips parted to expose a smile that was a bit too bright—almost forced—as Kyle and Eileen entered.

"We're looking for Michael Downum." Kyle wished then that he had a business card to offer, but he had none.

"Whom shall I say is looking?" The woman's expression turned guarded, protective. Eileen extended her hand and the young woman shook it quickly.

"My name is Eileen Caldwell, I have reason to believe Mr. Downum had business with my brother Jack."

The blonde blinked, then took a backward step.

"Ms. Downum."

"Pardon me?" Eileen frowned.

The blonde patted her chest. "I'm Michael Downum. Ms. Downum." She glanced from side to side to make sure they were alone. "I heard about your brother and I'm sorry. I liked Jack. He listened to me."

A few moments later they'd moved to a corner table. Michael had asked another waitress to cover the hostess desk, though based on the number of empty tables inside the restaurant, business was far from booming.

"How long have you worked here?" Kyle asked.

"Five years." The young woman answered in a voice that suggested she'd once been a smoker, though based on her luminous skin and lack of wrinkles, if she had smoked, she'd quit long ago.

Eileen leaned forward. "We won't waste your time,

Ms. Downum. We realize you're working—"

"Please call me Michael," the other woman interrupted, "and if I can help you find Jack, this is one interruption I'm happy to blow my break on."

"You said he listened to you?" Kyle did his best to come across as nonthreatening. He realized he tended to look anything but, yet Michael Downum was unaffected by his appearance. Perhaps she was used to a rougher crowd.

"Fifteen years ago my best friend and I were kidnapped." Her gaze widened as if the statement still surprised her. "I escaped and she didn't. But no one believed me. We weren't exactly good kids, if you know what I mean."

She tipped her head from side to side. "Sure, we ran with the wrong crowd and we liked to cut class, but did we deserve to get kidnapped and tossed into some cold room with nothing but a dirt floor? I don't think so."

"Did you go to the police?" Eileen asked.

Michael nodded dramatically. "Did I ever. They made me take a lie detector test and I failed miserably." She shrugged. "I've always been a bit on the high-strung side."

"And your friend?" Kyle prompted.

Michael's features turned sad. "Karen. Her name was Karen." She grew silent for a moment, visibly fighting the moisture gathering in her eyes. "I never saw her again. No one did."

"What did the police make of that?" Kyle leaned closer, appalled at the way the local authorities had apparently treated this young woman.

Michael drew in a deep breath before she spoke. "They classified her as a runaway, and then they washed their hands of the whole thing." She dropped her voice low. "But I'm not the only one who escaped. There are three of us. And we all got out of the same hellhole."

"Three?" Kyle and Eileen spoke simultaneously.

Michael nodded. "I'd convinced the other two to meet with Jack, but he never showed for our meeting."

The plot thickened, and how, Kyle thought. "When was this meeting?"

"Friday night," Michael answered. "Nine o'clock. He'd never stood me up before. I should have known something had happened to him."

The same evening Jack had planned to meet Eileen, and the night he'd vanished. Perhaps his abductor had decided to make a bold move before all hell broke loose.

"So you don't believe the suicide theory?" Eileen asked softly.

Michael's pale brows snapped together. "Hell, no. He was so close to blowing this kidnapping ring wide open, he could taste it. Everyone thought the Basso thing was his big deal, but this...this would have been huge."

And someone had gotten to him before he could go public.

Kyle pushed to his feet, shaking Michael's hand as he did so. "You've been a big help, thanks."

"There's one other thing I think you should know." She frowned slightly, as if she wasn't sure she should say whatever it was she was about to say. "Jack changed after I showed him where I escaped. The woods." She nodded. "For some reason it affected him. He was never the same after that day."

"Depressed?" Kyle asked.

"That's just it." Michael shook her head from side to side. "He wasn't depressed at all. He was angry."

"Would you take us there?" Eileen's bold question took Kyle by surprise. If she worked with the team long enough, she'd become a natural investigator.

Another nod. "My shift ends in an hour. Can you wait for me? The food is good, even though you'd never guess it by how empty it is in here. I'll take you to the spot I showed Jack, the spot where I escaped."

"One more question." Kyle reached for Michael's arm as she turned to walk away. "The other two women who escaped, did they go to the cops?"

The young woman shook her head.

"Why not?"

"He said he'd kill our families."

"Who's he?"

She shook her head again. "We never saw his face."

"Would you know his voice?" Kyle asked, fighting the anger growing inside him for what this young woman and countless others had been put through.

She nodded.

"Why weren't you afraid of his threats?" Eileen asked gently.

"No reason to be," Michael answered. "I was abandoned at birth." She gave a shrug that belied the pain in her young eyes. "Never had any family to kill."

TWO HOURS LATER, Eileen and Kyle stood in the midst of a dense forest. Michael had insisted on driving her car separately so that she could show them the spot and leave, not wanting to linger in a place that held such horrible memories for her.

Eileen could understand why.

The small hairs at the back of her scalp pricked to attention.

Kidnapping. Prostitution. Bold escapes.

Surely this wasn't the Pittsburgh she knew—or wanted to know—but chances were it was the Pittsburgh Jack had known.

His work on the U.S. Attorney's special task force had included human trafficking, yet Eileen had never guessed how close to home the illegal network operated.

"Do you know where we are exactly?" Kyle asked.

Eileen held out her hand. "Give me that GPS unit Martin gave you."

"Gadgets," he mumbled under his breath as he shook his head and walked away. "I must have left it somewhere."

Eileen frowned then tipped her chin to study the sky above her, spotting nothing but branches and leaves, as if the blue of sky had been replaced by green.

Kyle paced away from her, looking for a trapdoor or some sign of an underground passageway, but Eileen focused on their surroundings.

The route they'd taken while following Michael had been eerily familiar to the route Eileen had taken earlier that day on her way to her family's farm. She hadn't been out to the edges of the massive property since Robert's disappearance, but she remembered the general location.

The knot in the pit of her stomach suggested her instincts agreed with her memory for once. She and Kyle were standing on Caldwell property. She recognized their surroundings enough to know she didn't need a GPS unit to provide her with proof.

Had a facility on Caldwell land once used for running booze been used to house kidnap victims en route to an illegal sex trade?

Her mother's notes had been detailed as far as numbers of women and cargo handled, but she'd never named names, and she hadn't been specific about locations.

Disbelief and denial tangled inside her.

Her family history couldn't contain such horror, could it?

Yet, if Michael Downum had been correct in bringing them here, the underground prison from which Michael and the two other women had escaped had been on her family's property.

Her grandfather had been alive fifteen years ago, so the grim truth was that his involvement was possible, yet it wasn't likely. He'd been in failing health toward the end of his life.

So who had run the operation?

Had Jack been closing in on the truth? Had it gotten

him abducted? Or worse?

"Anything?" Kyle called out from several yards away.

Eileen thought about lying, but she and Kyle had shared too much for her to take that backward step now. She nodded and he was at her side instantly, studying her carefully.

"This is my family's land." Resignation settled over her. "Michael was kidnapped and held hostage on my family's property."

Kyle anchored an arm around her as if he feared her shock might finally overtake her.

"She said your brother was angry. I suppose learning something like this went on behind your back could do that to you."

Eileen gathered herself, trying to focus on why they'd come here. To find the spot. To find the room.

"Did you find anything?" she asked.

But Kyle merely shook his head. "Ground cover is too dense and Michael said she never fully remembered climbing out of a room or passageway, she only remembered waking up in the leaves."

Shock and remorse tangled inside Eileen. "So now what?"

Kyle started walking, urging Eileen back toward the clearing where they'd parked their car.

"So now we head back to the team and we let Silvia do one of her favorite things."

"Such as?"

"Tap into her favorite thermal satellite program."

CHAPTER FOURTEEN

Body Clock: 82:55

I t was shortly before midnight when Kyle returned from his run. A light still glowed from
Eileen's window and he sensed her pain, even
though she hadn't said much of anything since
Michael had taken them to the Caldwell property.

The team had instantly gone into action, working
the long hours since he and Eileen had returned to the
house. Silvia's search and download of thermal imaging for the region had turned up nothing, but she'd
left the program running, scanning the grid, just in
case something changed.

The region's dense foliage was more than likely a
deterrent to the satellite's range and effectiveness.

Maggie and Martin had continued to sort through
Betty Caldwell's documentation and photographs,

cataloguing information by date, hoping for a link to DiMauro or Basso, anything that might explain both Robert and Jack Caldwell's fixation on what they'd discovered.

Of course, the team was working on the theory Robert Caldwell had stumbled upon the documentation prior to his disappearance. Other than proof of the illegal human trade conducted within the lines of the Caldwell property, theory was all the Body Hunters had at this point.

In addition to searching thermal imaging, Silvia had set to work enhancing a number of the old photographs found at the farm, particularly those in which the same dark-haired man appeared over and over.

Eileen had felt the man was neither her grandfather nor her father, yet she'd been unable to explain her feeling she knew him from somewhere.

Chances were fairly strong she'd met the man when she'd been just a child and while his identity hadn't clung to her memory, his image had. Perhaps with a refinement and enlargement of the photos, she'd be able to tap into a name she'd thought long forgotten.

Kyle headed for her room now and knocked softly, not wanting to wake her on the off chance she'd fallen asleep with the lights on.

When she answered the door, pain and shock glazed her red-rimmed eyes. Kyle could think of nothing but erasing the hurt and cushioning the shock she'd experienced.

Finding Jack was still the team's priority, but Eileen had moved front and center in Kyle's mind. He found himself thinking about her, worrying about her, wondering about her each moment she wasn't by his side.

The woman had not only gotten under his skin, but she'd also begun to burrow deep into his heart.

"Don't you ever sleep?" she asked, her smile forced, not fooling him for a moment.

As he studied her fragile expression, he understood exactly why he'd come to her room tonight. Not to hold her, not to listen to her breath at sleep.

He'd come here to be with her, fully, as he'd wanted to be with her since the first time he saw her in Cielo.

EILEEN'S HEART beat in her throat as Kyle stepped into her room and shut and locked the door behind him.

"Would you rather I left you alone tonight?" he asked, his eyes shining with concern.

She shook her head, amazed at how much comfort his arrival provided.

Her brain hadn't yet been able to process what they'd discovered today. From her mother's notes and photographs to Michael's firsthand description of the horrors she'd endured, Eileen thought her spirit would surely break beneath the reality of her family's past.

Eileen thought again about how visibly upset Kyle had been with her today. While she'd first been touched by his concern, she'd since begun to consider another option.

Had he been bothered by the fact she'd put herself

in danger's way potentially, or had he been upset by the possibility he'd miss a vital clue by not being by her side?

While she hoped for the former, smart money said she needed to consider the latter.

"I'm sorry I didn't let you know where I was going today. I'd never do anything to jeopardize your case."

Kyle blinked, a genuinely stunned expression crossing his face. "Do you honestly think I was upset about the case?" He reached for her, his strong fingers caressing her upper arms. "I was upset about you. Worried about your safety."

Her breath caught and she glanced down, unable to meet head-on the intensity of what he'd just said.

Kyle moved one hand to her chin, lifting her face to his.

"I care about *you*." He spoke the words tentatively, as if he hadn't said them aloud to anyone in a very long time.

Based on their conversation from the night before, she imagined he hadn't.

Suddenly, her every concern about Kyle Landenburg's intentions evaporated.

She reached out a hand to graze his cheek, stunned when he moved suddenly, pulling her fully into his arms and against his chest with such force the air rushed from her lungs.

His lips crushed hers, and her body responded instantly.

Need and desire spiked to life inside her, and she could no longer fight how much she wanted this strong man.

Kyle tunneled his fingers through her hair, pulling her face even more tightly to his, nipping at her lower lip.

Heat built inside her, low and heavy, and she pressed her body to his, wanting him inside her as she'd never wanted anything.

But Kyle had other plans.

He walked them toward the bed, never breaking their kiss or the erotic dance of hands to bodies. The back of her knees hit the bed and she gasped, dropping to sit as he dropped to his knees on the floor.

He tugged at the sweater she wore, sliding it up and over her head as she wiggled her arms free. The sweater snagged on the clip she'd shoved into her hair and as she struggled to release herself, Kyle's incredible hands palmed her breasts, testing their weight.

Eileen pulled the sweater free of her hair and lowered her stare to his, their eyes locking. Breathlessness pulsed through her even though the man had done nothing more than peel off one article of her clothing.

"Amazing," he said softly, and she was lost.

Kyle pulled the lace of her bra aside, exposing first one breast and then the other, drinking her in with his eyes. The moment was more erotic than anything she'd ever known...until he lowered his mouth to the valley between her breasts, cupping her with his hands, suckling, teasing, tasting.

She squirmed beneath his touch, willing her body to maintain control when she knew her control had vanished the moment he'd pressed his lips to her bare flesh.

Kyle reached to unclasp her bra, slid it free of her arms, then reached for her face, studying her again, his eyes so dark they'd gone bottomless and black.

She searched for something to say, something meaningful or sexy, but could think of nothing, nothing but how the jolt of Kyle's touch had brought her to life on a day when she'd thought nothing could bring her back again.

He reached for the waist of her slacks, unsnapping the closure and tugging the zipper lower and lower still, removing the barrier with ease.

She leaned back on her hands, letting him undress her, inhaling sharply when he slipped two fingers beneath the elastic edge of her panties and tested the feel of her, dipping first one finger and then the other inside her.

Her release began to build—a slow, steady heat humming to life, dulling her senses, her focus, everything but the sensation of Kyle's touch. He removed her panties, lowered his mouth to her, and did not disappoint.

Mind-numbing pleasure fired to life inside her, and she told herself to feel. Nothing more.

And so she did, focusing on the heat of his mouth as he alternated between teasing and tasting, his fingers stroking deep inside her.

Eileen gripped his shoulders and squeezed, biting back a moan as her orgasm splintered through her, blinding her with crackling sensations of electricity and release.

Then Kyle broke contact, moving like a wild animal, shedding his clothing—shirt, jeans, underwear—before Eileen could so much as catch her breath. He reached his hands between her legs and pulled her toward him, sliding inside her with an intensity that stole her breath.

She'd often wondered what the man would be like should his bottled emotions and intense spirit find a way to escape his protective walls, and now she knew.

He slid his hands to her bottom, pulling her so tightly to him she thought she might shatter. Another orgasm had begun its mesmerizing dance around the periphery of her awareness when he thrust into her, harder now.

They moved as one and Eileen felt her body tighten around Kyle, pulsing with her release, this one even more intense than her first.

She fell back onto the bed and as Kyle shifted fully on top of her, she anchored her legs around his hips and held on for the ride.

KYLE MOVED inside Eileen faster than he'd intended to, but the feel of her wrapped around him—around his erection—was more than he could take. He'd always been the one to set the pace while making love, but in this case, the glow of Eileen's skin, the sound of her excited breathing, and the feel of her body's release was more than he could take.

She controlled him, whether she knew it or not.

When she dropped back onto the bed and took him

even more fully inside her, his vision began to dim, his release building until he thought he might cry out. She anchored her legs around his hips and trailed her touch up the length of his belly to his bare chest, raking a fingernail across each nipple.

Kyle lost control instantly, his orgasm exploding in a release of pent-up emotion, need, and desire.

Their bodies pulsed together and he felt her reach yet another orgasm, this one smaller, yet intense.

Eileen's eyes closed and the corners of her mouth curved into a gentle smile. She wrapped her fingers around his neck, pulling her to him.

He studied her, amazed the creature before him truly was real…here, with him.

But when she blinked her eyes open and stared at him so intently he could have sworn she looked into the depths of his soul, Kyle realized Eileen was not only real, she was the most incredible woman he'd ever known.

Their lovemaking left him wrung dry, more physically spent than any run ever could. He knew his body was strong enough to take the exertion, but was his heart?

He lowered himself gently on top of her, rolling onto his back to pull her beside him. She draped one arm over his chest and nuzzled her head into the space between his shoulder and neck. The musky smell of their lovemaking wrapped its fingers around Kyle's brain and dulled his senses, relaxing him fully.

Not for the first time during the past few days, he wondered how he'd ever go back to Seattle and leave

Eileen behind. He knew he wouldn't ask her to go with him, not when she'd made her desire to stay and make things right with her brother so clear during their shared confidences. And he couldn't imagine himself staying here in Pittsburgh. His life was in Seattle, not that many people would call it a life.

He shoved the train of thought from his brain and willed himself to stay in the moment—this moment —with Eileen. He'd made love with a beautiful, intelligent woman who'd come to occupy his every waking moment, and Kyle intended to enjoy what they'd found together.

The morning would bring back reality soon enough, but he intended to savor the feel of her satiny skin next to his, the length of her slender leg pressed to his, the weight of her arm across his chest, the warmth of her breath against his neck.

For now, he wanted nothing more than to lie here with Eileen, secure in the knowledge neither of them wanted to be anywhere else.

For the second time in as many nights, sleep pushed at the edges of his awareness, winning the battle between his visions and his exhaustion.

As he slipped ever deeper toward slumber, he thought again about tomorrow then decided something vital.

Tomorrow could wait.

CHAPTER FIFTEEN

Body Clock: 89:15

D aylight peeked around the edges of the bedroom's curtains when Eileen woke. She rolled onto her side, admiring the way the sheet draped across Kyle's bare chest. Even in his sleep, his face held on to traces of the tension she'd expected their lovemaking to relieve.

Her body hummed in places it had never hummed, her every muscle satiated, yet spent.

A songbird's cry filled the morning outside, and Eileen slipped from beneath the covers and pulled Kyle's sweatshirt over her head, breathing deep of his purely male, musky scent.

Deep inside her, her body called out for more —more caresses, more quietly whispered promises, more Kyle.

She pressed a featherweight kiss to his forehead then tiptoed to the bathroom, taking great care not to wake him. She knew his dreams were typically the place where his visions pursued him, but based on his sound sleep, perhaps last night had been the night to break his psyche's hold on him.

She hoped so.

A few moments later, she'd freshened up and pulled on a pair of jeans. Still wearing Kyle's sweatshirt for warmth, she grabbed the sunglasses from her bureau and her cell phone, determined to spend a few quiet moments outside in the beautiful early morning sun.

Voices sounded from down the hall, filtering up from the case room. She could picture the scene—Silvia simultaneously working on Jack's quilt and running thermal satellite scans of the area in and around the Caldwell family farm, Martin digging deep into the topic of human trafficking and looking for a link between the Caldwell family and DiMauro or Basso, Maggie sorting through Betty Caldwell's notes.

The moment Eileen stepped outside, everything in the house faded away.

Just like the sheer release of making love to Kyle last night, the beauty of the morning carried Eileen away from the reality of her life—both brothers missing and her family history like nothing she could have ever imagined. She'd been born and raised in the midst of unthinkable evil, yet she hadn't had a clue.

Had Robert? Had Jack?

More than likely they'd both made the same discovery, and for each the knowledge of their family's past had brought about a downward spiral into depression and obsession. Would Eileen do the same?

She strolled down the hill away from the house toward the property's pond, admiring the grouping of geese that had yet to depart for warmer climates. She dropped to the grass, pulling her knees to her chin and hugging her legs.

If only she could stay here forever in this moment, the happy fog of being with Kyle numbing the pain of the past and the present.

Her cell phone vibrated in the pocket of Kyle's sweatshirt and she swore softly beneath her breath. So much for undisturbed quiet time.

She glanced down at the phone's display window.

Patrick O'Malley.

No doubt he wanted to personally blame her for Henry's death and whatever other trauma The Body Hunters investigation had inflicted on his precious department.

But she couldn't have been more wrong.

"It's time you knew the truth." He spoke the words without emotion when she answered the phone.

"Such as?" An odd sense of suspicion tapped at the base of Eileen's brain. Perhaps Kyle's lecture on taking chances had hit its intended mark, or perhaps the last few days had taken their toll, but she found herself unable to be anything but defensive and wary when it came to Patrick.

"Meet me at the overlook."

Now that she hadn't expected.

Eileen scowled at the phone. "What on earth for?"

"Because the spot has meaning for what I'm about to tell you and you need to come alone. This is family business. Family history."

The familiar argument burned inside her, longing to get out. Hers was not Patrick's family. He'd inserted himself into their lives and he'd stuck, like a thorn in their collective sides.

"Are you still there?"

She nodded. "What time?"

"I'm on my way there now. I'll be waiting for you."

She couldn't help but feel a bit indignant. "Pretty confident I'd say yes, weren't you?"

"You never could say no to new information or the answer to one of your damned questions, Eileen. It's what made me love you like the daughter I never had."

His words lingered long after Eileen ended the call.

Never in all the years she'd known Patrick O'Malley had he referred to her as much more than a pain in the ass. Now he was calling her the daughter he never had?

What on earth was going on?

She glanced at the house as she headed for her car, knowing she'd left her keys under the mat last night. She'd picked up the habit on Cielo where the crime was low. While she'd never find her car waiting for her if she did the same in the city, she'd figured she was safe doing so here at the secluded Body Hunters compound.

She stepped beneath the heavy tree canopy and slid the sunglasses from her face in order to see. She realized her mistake instantly. She'd grabbed Martin's spy glasses instead of her own, but she didn't want to risk waking Kyle by going back inside.

She'd make do with these, and with any luck at all, she'd return with the key to the entire puzzle, or at least enough information to help Kyle forgive her for what she was about to do—sneak off on her own again.

She'd be lying if she didn't admit the thought made her nervous, but if she didn't do as Patrick had instructed, she might never learn whatever it was he wanted to tell her. And as much as she wanted to include Kyle, she couldn't risk making a move that might cost Jack his freedom...or worse.

KYLE WASN'T SURE how long he'd been asleep before the dream's images assaulted him, flashing through his mind, hitting him so hard he woke breathless.

The woman ran, struggling, crashing to her knees, panicked and in fear for her life.

She'd been surrounded by trees just as in previous versions of the vision, but this time, there was a crucial difference.

As her pursuer drew nearer, ever nearer, she turned, facing Kyle full on. And this time, she wasn't faceless at all.

Kyle forced himself awake, sitting bolt upright in bed, alone.

A dent in Eileen's pillow was the only trace she'd left behind. Kyle was on his feet and into his jeans as fast as humanly possible. Then he was running, down the hall and out the front door, swearing beneath his breath at the sight that greeted him.

Eileen was gone. Her car was gone. But to where?

He raced back inside and pounded down the stairs and into the case room. As he'd hoped, Martin sat deep in thought, still working the puzzle of the research the archive boxes had presented.

The second computer continued to process and enhance the photographs they'd pulled from the documentation...enlarging, sharpening, refining.

And then he saw it. The familiar profile clear as day but more than twenty years younger—the man he'd met and disliked instantly.

Adrenaline spiked to life in Kyle's veins. He'd thought himself wide-awake before, but his sense of urgency kicked his every sense to a higher level of activity.

"Son of a—" Kyle whistled.

"Patrick O'Malley." Will spoke from behind Kyle as if he couldn't believe his eyes. "Where's the rest of the team?"

"Worked late. No one's moving yet," Martin answered.

"Eileen's gone." Panic tapped at the base of Kyle's brain. "We have to locate her, and fast."

He'd believed Eileen when she'd promised him she wouldn't pull another stunt, wouldn't take off again without him, and yet she had.

He'd be lying if he didn't admit the betrayal hurt. But as he stared at the picture of the much younger Patrick O'Malley, entrenched in the kidnapping ring documented by Eileen's mother, he understood exactly what would have made Eileen break her word.

The promise of the truth.

The promise of a lead in finding Jack, and perhaps finding Robert.

Kyle knew exactly who had called her away.

And now he had to find her and save her, before it was too late.

"I need you trace my GPS unit." Kyle found himself breathless, filled with the unfamiliar sense of being out of control, when he prided himself on being anything but.

Martin twisted up his features. "But you're standing right in front of me."

"Can you trace my GPS or not?"

Martin's fingers flew across the keys, and a stationery beacon flashed on a map a split second later. "There." The younger operative pointed to the screen, and Kyle leaned in to read the location, the bottom falling out of his stomach as the recognition set in.

"She's gone to the overlook." Kyle pushed away from the monitor, headed for the steps. "Patrick O'Malley is playing both sides." Kyle pointed at the enhanced image on the computer screen. "Apparently he has been for a long time."

"I'll alert the rest of the team." Will gripped Kyle's arm as they passed each other. "Call me the second you get there. We'll be ready for whatever needs to be done."

"The GPS isn't moving," Martin called out after him.

"But we are," Will answered. "Get the rest of

the communicators ready and pull one for yourself. You're going into the field. Silvia can stay behind to track us once we're on the move."

But Kyle didn't hear any more. Within seconds, he was on the move, speeding toward the Majestic Overlook, hoping against hope she'd be there and be unharmed when he arrived.

His intuition had come to life, gnawing a hole in the pit of his stomach—a hole that suggested he was about to walk into his worst nightmare.

He'd ignored the recurring vision, shoving it from his waking mind time after time. And just like the image that might have saved Sally years earlier, this image might have saved Eileen.

If only he'd paid attention.

THE PRODUCER sat in the backseat of the large SUV, shielded by the heavily tinted windows. He watched as the familiar car approached. Eileen Caldwell.

His men were in position waiting to make their move.

The Producer had broken the news to Jack this morning, not that Caldwell had understood. He'd slipped into unconsciousness sometime during the night and his recovery was looking a bit doubtful at this point. No matter. As long as the Caldwell sister delivered, the Producer would have all he wanted.

It wasn't as though he planned to let either of the Caldwell siblings live. After all, he'd never been a fan of leaving a potential witness behind.

The woman pulled her car to a stop and climbed

out of the door, scanning her surroundings. Her gaze settled on the SUV, her expression puzzled, but she headed toward the overlook, as the Producer knew O'Malley had instructed her to do.

More than likely, she thought the man was delayed and still on his way.

Wasn't she in for a shock?

She walked confidently toward the overlook, casually dressed, hair tousled, definitely not the put-together woman he'd witnessed here just yesterday. She pulled off a pair of sunglasses and hooked them onto the neck of her oversized sweatshirt.

If the Producer didn't know better, he'd say she had the glow of a woman who had just gotten lucky in love.

He laughed as the bulky figures of his men emerged from the stand of trees off to the side of where Caldwell waited, sitting casually on one of the overlook benches.

Lucky in love, she might be, but her lucky-in-life quotient had just run out.

The Producer laced his fingers behind his head, sat back against the seat and prepared to enjoy the show.

CHAPTER SIXTEEN

Body Clock: 90:25

U nease simmered to life inside Eileen's gut. Patrick should have been here before her. The drive to the overlook was shorter from downtown than it was from the safe house. Perhaps he'd had an emergency, or been delayed somehow.

She should have checked her cell phone to make sure she hadn't missed a call due to a dropped signal —not uncommon in this region—but she'd left her phone back in the car.

If he didn't show in the next few minutes, she'd go back and check for missed calls, but in the meantime, she might as well enjoy the beautiful morning as she'd been doing back at the pond.

Eileen had no sooner settled on a bench than she spotted movement in her peripheral vision.

As if a scene from a movie, two darkly dressed men emerged from a cluster of trees.

What on earth?

Then she remembered the SUV. Perhaps they'd parked and taken an early morning hike, though their outfits were fit for anything but.

She glanced back at the rushing water below, not wanting to stare at the men or draw their attention, but she needn't have worried. They walked casually back toward their SUV, not sparing so much as a glance in her direction.

Eileen pushed to her feet just the same, wanting to be able to move quickly should she need to. Her instinct proved to be spot-on.

The sound of running footfalls crunching across the gravel stunned her momentarily, until she realized the men had waited until they were directly behind her before they came at her.

Had Patrick set her up? Lured her into a trap?

She didn't wait for her mind to process the questions. Panic exploded through her, and she sprinted away from the bench toward the dense foliage, hoping she could move more quickly than the men and find a hiding spot.

She reached for the video glasses hooked on her sweatshirt and pressed the hinge as Martin had explained just as she crashed through the stand of trees, low branches tearing at her sweatshirt sleeves and jeans.

Her pursuers closed behind her.

Who were they? Was this how Jack had met his fate? Running from an unknown assailant, racing to survive?

As the large men crashed through the foliage behind her—far closer than she'd expected—dread and raw fear sliced through her.

She wasn't capable of outrunning the men. Short of going over the side of the ravine, she could only hope the camera was on and transmitting.

She stumbled, falling to her knees, her palms connecting with sharp rocks, pine needles and dirt.

Pain sliced through her, uncoiling from her right wrist upward.

Damn it.

She rolled onto her side then righted herself, trying desperately to pull herself to her knees. Willing her body to run, run, run.

But she was too late.

A hand shoved her to the ground and dirt and needles filled her nose and eyes.

She tried to crawl, tried to scramble away, but a crushing blow hit the back of her skull, followed quickly by a second.

And as she slid into unconsciousness, her gaze landed on the glasses, thrown free of her body, more than a foot away, pointed directly at her.

She mouthed a single word. A single name.

Kyle.

And as her world turned to black, she could only pray he got the message.

"WE'VE GOT A TRANSMISSION." The sound of Silvia's voice and the team communicator channel crackling to life jolted Kyle's system.

"Audio?" Will asked.

"Video." The older woman didn't wait for any additional questions or comments. "Eileen's in trouble and down."

Kyle swerved momentarily then righted his car. "What do you mean?" But the next voice Kyle heard wasn't Silvia's, it was Will's.

"She transmitted an image that could only have been taken with her running. She tore through trees, scrambling. And then she went down. It's bad, Kyle. The glasses must have been thrown. The last image is of her face, mouthing your name."

Will might as well have described Kyle's vision. "It is bad," he mumbled, just as he pulled into the overlook parking lot.

One car sat parked neatly in the parking area. Eileen's.

Unfortunately for Kyle, she was nowhere in sight.

"I'm here now. Her car appears deserted. Let me do a quick search and get back to you."

"Any idea on where O'Malley might have taken her?" Will asked.

Kyle had cleared his driver's door and sprinted toward Eileen's car. Wherever she'd been taken, her cell phone had been left behind, sitting forgotten in the center console of her car.

Just like her brothers before her, she'd vanished into thin air.

And Kyle had let it happen.

He'd failed a woman he loved. Again.

And he did love Eileen. He'd never been more sure of anything. He could only pray he'd have the chance to tell her.

"Kyle?" Will's voice.

And then a new vision hit Kyle. Hard.

A dirt floor. A bare room. Restraints.

This time, Kyle did something he'd fought so hard against in the past. He trusted the image, he launched himself into action based on nothing but raw instinct and belief.

"She's at the farm," he yelled into his communicator. "On the outskirts of the property." He rattled off the coordinates for the location Michael had shown them, hoping against hope his intuition wasn't lying.

And when he reached the secluded spot—unlike last night's failure to find a room, to find a trapdoor, anything—he'd have to find a way into the hellhole from which Patrick O'Malley had once operated.

EILEEN WOKE SLOWLY, face down on a cold, dirt floor.

The pain from her wrist sent a wave of nausea careening through her.

She blinked her eyes into focus, her gaze settling on another body, this one in far worse shape than hers.

Jack.

She recognized his unconscious form, even though his facial features were bloodied and swollen beyond recognition.

She crawled toward him, moving on her side, unable to use her right arm. She reached with her left, pulling herself forward, closer to the brother she feared she'd lost forever.

His chest rose slightly with a breath, then fell and rose again. Tears flooded her vision.

He was alive. He'd survived this long. Now she had only to get him out of this place and get him help.

Eileen gently brushed a lock of hair from his forehead, pain gripping her heart and squeezing tight.

What had she done by leaving him behind to face the hell of their family history alone? She should have been here. Here with Jack. Here with the truth.

She swallowed down her grief and shame and forced herself to focus. She was here now. She'd save him now, she had to.

"Jack." She pressed a kiss to his face. "Jack. It's Eileen. Can you hear me?"

His swollen eyes cracked open and his mouth moved. "Pro—Producer."

His eyes closed and Eileen pulled herself beside him, cradling him gently. "Come on, Jack. Stay with me. Talk to me."

Her brother's pale eyes opened again, a flicker of determination visible beneath his lashes. "Ro—Rob…"

She feared what he was about to say even as he struggled, unable to force the words from his lips.

The very thought their older brother might have played a role in Jack's abduction tilted Eileen's world on its axis.

But the puzzle pieces flew through her mind, suddenly making sense.

Her intruder's vivid eyes.

The history of kidnappings dating back to her grandfather's days.

Their farm and its gruesome past.

Robert's suspected meetings with DiMauro, Basso and, potentially, Ferdinand King.

"Robert?" she asked.

"Actually, I prefer the name Producer. After all, it's what I do. I make things happen."

Robert's voice slammed Eileen like a blast from the past. The horror of the completed puzzle hit her as she stared up into Robert's blue eyes—vivid, but ice-cold. Yet his features weren't what she remembered. They'd been altered, shifted, reshaped.

"Cosmetic surgery." He shrugged even as he pointed a gun at her face. "The physicians in Europe are quite gifted. It's amazing what money can buy." He gave a sharp laugh. "You never could mind your own business, could you?"

"What have you done?" she asked.

"The correct question—" he shrugged "—would be what have you done? And more importantly, what are you going to do to fix it?"

KYLE REACHED the farm in record time, following his memory to find the same clearing where he'd parked last night.

He climbed from his car, standing for a moment without moving, trying to get his bearings. Trying to conjure up the images from the vision he'd had back at the overlook.

His mind had gone blank except for one thing—the image of Eileen's face.

If he failed to find her, he'd never forgive himself,

never be able to face himself in the mirror again. Hell, if he failed Eileen, his life would be even emptier than it had been before, now that he'd experienced what life with her could be like.

"Kyle." Silvia's voice sounded in his communicator. "I have you in my sights and I have even better news than that."

Kyle squeezed his eyes shut momentarily, hoping against hope the computer whiz was about to say what he'd hope she'd say.

"The thermal satellite's giving me an image."

Kyle's gut tightened. "Where?" he growled, urgency firing inside him.

"Two hundred yards, south southwest."

Kyle glanced down at his watch and adjusted his direction, moving as fast as he could through the dense foliage and underbrush.

"Perfect." Silvia's voice rang out. "The team's on their way. For God's sake, be careful, and bring them home."

He'd no sooner slowed his motion, guessing he'd covered the ground necessary, when his communicator chirped to life again.

This time, Silvia whispered. "You're literally right on top of the chamber."

And then Kyle spotted what he'd been unable to spot yesterday—a break in the dense brush. He moved slowly, not wanting to alert anyone who might be in the chamber beneath him.

A steel door, similar to what one might find on a ship, sat framed by foliage. A camouflage tarp had been tossed to one side.

Whoever was using the chamber was here now, of that Kyle was sure.

He dropped to his hands and knees, pulling a listening device from his pocket and pressing it against the metal.

What he heard made his blood run cold.

He strained to isolate voices, zeroing in instantly on Eileen's, but a second voice threw him.

Who could it be? A member of the Basso family? Or Eileen's brother, Jack?

Kyle listened another moment, taking in the hateful verbiage being tossed about.

Anger seethed inside him, but he fought to maintain control. He had to, if he wanted to save Eileen. And he had every intention of saving her.

This time, he would not fail.

Silvia had said the team was on their way, but Kyle couldn't afford to wait. Eileen's life depended on his decision and actions.

Kyle took a deep breath, readied himself mentally and prepared to make his move.

EILEEN CONTINUED to cradle Jack's broken body, unable to believe one brother could have inflicted such pain on another.

Robert was in the middle of his bragging session on how he'd masterminded everything from his own disappearance and new life in Europe to faking Jack's suicide.

It took every ounce of restraint Eileen possessed

not to fly at the bastard she'd once called big brother and pound her fists into his face. How could she have lived with and grown up with the heartless man and not have recognized Robert for what he was?

Pure evil.

"Our handwriting is almost identical, so the note wasn't a problem," Robert explained. "As best I can tell, the investigation was over almost before it began."

"Not exactly." Eileen couldn't help herself, she couldn't stay silent any longer.

"Your friends at the farmhouse?" Robert asked. "They don't worry me."

"That's funny." Eileen faked a bravado she in no way felt. "They were up all night combing through the documentation of the kidnappings. The truth will come out, with or without me."

That got Robert's attention.

But the next voice Eileen heard wasn't Robert's at all.

"Correction. As usual." Patrick stepped through the doorway and Eileen's stomach pitched sideways. "Around here I control the truth." He shook his head. "Your little investigation stops here. And to think, if you'd only kept your nose out of it, all of this could have been avoided."

Eileen breathed in sharply, and Jack stirred in her arms.

She stroked his forehead and willed him to stay still. He couldn't take another beating and there was no telling what Patrick or Robert had planned for either of them.

"I've spent a lifetime perfecting my position." Patrick paced to where Eileen sat holding Jack and pushed at Jack's side with the toes of his shoe.

Eileen reached for his foot, slapping his shoe away. "Robert was always so like me that he naturally wanted to follow in my footsteps, but you and Jack. You both insisted on the truth." He made a tsking noise with his mouth. "So much like your mother. Did you know your brother Jack honestly thought he could take down the likes of Richie Basso and Nicholas DiMauro as well as me?"

"So they're all involved?" She asked the question she'd asked before, hoping this time Patrick would give her an answer.

He did.

"Yes, they're involved. Does that make you happy? With their combined infrastructures in distribution and real estate, we've set up illegal brothels all over the world. There's no stopping us."

He spit on the floor next to Jack.

"No stopping us at all."

Patrick's comment about her mother tangled in her brain with the date of the last journal entry she and the team had found.

"Did you kill our mother to keep her quiet?"

Surprise lit in Patrick's eyes, but he gave no response. Instead he continued with his diatribe, perhaps wanting to reward her with all of the answers she'd craved before either he or Robert silenced her for good.

"Your grandfather was never in favor of the use of his property for our work. But after your parents' accident he realized cooperation was the only way to ensure a financially secure future for the three of you." He patted his chest. "And I'd never wanted anything but that."

Eileen shook her head. "You never cared about my family. You used my family, and you killed our parents. You killed them to stop my mother from going public with her records and photographs, and you killed them to blackmail my grandfather into cooperating with you."

Eileen was right and she knew it, especially when Patrick began to nod.

"You always were smart," he said. "Too smart. Not like your brothers. They merely did what I said, at least until Jack decided to play hardball." He laughed and the sound chilled Eileen to the bone. "But just look at how far that got him."

Patrick pivoted on his heel. "Look at Robert. Sure, he had to change his face a bit, but did he tell you he's the head of our entire European operation now? The day he disappeared was the day he started his new life —his real life."

But something had shifted in Robert's expression, and Eileen decided to make her move. "His real life was here, with us, with his parents—before you took them away from us."

"No." Patrick shook his head. "I spent a lifetime building and protecting my legacy and now it's Robert's turn to enjoy the money and the connections."

Eileen's stomach turned, her insides going liquid. The man was mad. Nothing she could say would get through to him.

She'd have to focus her efforts on Robert.

But even as the thought went through her mind, a loud noise sounded from the other side of the door and Kyle charged through the opening, tackling Robert and taking him to his knees.

Patrick moved with lightning speed, slamming his own weapon with a sickening thud into the side of Kyle's head. Kyle dropped, his six-foot-four, solidly muscled frame going limp.

Her heart caught in her throat, raw fear and shock gripping her and holding tight.

Robert dragged him to a corner, and waved his gun. "Let's get this over with already. Enough."

Patrick's gun had fallen from his hand, but he made no move to retrieve it, apparently feeling invincible.

"We have nothing to fear from this man. He more than likely thought he could play the white knight to your sister here. We have plenty of time. Try to remember who calls the shots around here. It isn't you."

Robert's brow furrowed. "It isn't me? I've handled every piece of footwork in this operation from kidnapping my own brother to killing that big-mouthed bartender. Why shouldn't it be me who gives the orders?"

From the corner of her eye, Eileen saw Kyle stir. His eyes opened slightly and their gazes met and held. She shook her head, wanting him to stay put, not wanting the next blow he took to be his last. Together they could find a way out of this alive.

Robert was beginning to crack, she only needed to find a way to hasten the process.

"Arrange for me to get those journals, Eileen, and I'll let you go," Patrick said.

"Why?" Jack stirred and Eileen pulled him more closely to her. "So you can destroy the only evidence against you?"

"*Eileen.*" She recognized the impatient tone.

Patrick's shiny veneer was beginning to splinter apart.

"You'll never let me go. You'll never let Jack go. You're going to kill us both because we don't serve your purpose." She pointed at Robert. "And don't think you're immune just because you changed your face and call yourself the Producer. He'll kill you as soon as spit on you if you make a wrong move."

Patrick's next statement came from out of the blue.

"I loved your mother."

Eileen could barely believe her ears. What was the man talking about? "My mother loved my father."

His smile made her blood run cold. "You never knew your mother."

"Why? Because I was just a child when you *murdered* her?"

"She was about to destroy everything I'd worked for." He spoke the words as if his justification were perfectly normal.

Kyle had begun a slow crawl away from the corner of the room. Eileen had the full attention of both Patrick and Robert, and if she could hold their focus a few moments longer, Kyle would be in position to grab Patrick's gun.

"You just said you loved her." Eileen shook her head.

"Sometimes life is about making difficult choices."

"Why Jack?"

"He asked too many questions," Patrick answered.

"That's funny. I thought that's what you paid him to do."

"Not when they concern my past."

"And your life of crime?"

Patrick stepped closer. Her skin crawled at the thought he might touch her.

"You and I," he said in barely more than a whisper, "are more alike than you'll ever know."

"We're nothing alike." Eileen held his stare, determined not to be the one who looked away first, determined to give Kyle ample time to reach the gun.

"I've always said you were the spitting image of your mother, but it's hard to say whether you inherited the fire in your belly from your mother or your father."

"My father was a gentle man, and apparently an innocent victim."

"Was he?" Patrick laughed. "You have no idea of who your real father is."

He winked, something she had never seen Patrick O'Malley do. She bit back the bile in her throat.

What was he trying to say? That he was her father?

She thought about how different she'd always been

from her brothers and felt herself go numb momentarily. Could her mother have had an affair with Patrick O'Malley? An affair that had resulted in Eileen's birth?

Or had the affair ended with Betty Caldwell's discovery of Patrick's heinous crimes?

"What the hell is the matter with you?" Robert's sharp tone drew Patrick's scrutiny away from Eileen. "Leave her alone."

"Since when have I ever let you tell me what to do?"

"She's my sister."

"Is she?"

Robert and Eileen locked stares. Emotions warred in her brother's face and Eileen realized her best chance to get through to him was now.

"Don't do this, Robert. Please."

Something in his eyes cracked, and a sliver of the past escaped, a light she hadn't seen there since they were children.

"You were in my house, weren't you?" Her heart twisted and her every last ounce of pride drained from her body. If she had to beg to save Jack, to save Kyle, to save herself, she would.

"I heard you call my name," she continued. "I saw your eyes. You moved the frame, didn't you? Our family. *Family*, Robert. We're family—you, me and Jack. We're all we have left. Don't do this."

"Shoot her," Patrick instructed. "This has grown tiresome."

"What about the documents?" Robert asked.

And Eileen knew then that the documents truly

were the cause of everything, from her parents' death to Jack's abduction.

"I'll destroy them," she said. "I'll go back and I'll burn every last sheet of paper. Every photo. Just let Jack go. Let me get him the medical attention he needs."

"Shoot her," Patrick repeated. "Shoot them all. Enough."

Robert continued to stare at Eileen, their gazes locked, the corners of his eyes softening ever so slightly at her words.

"He killed our parents, Robert," she said. "He's not the father figure you think he is. He took our father from us. He killed them, Robert. He's made you no better than he is."

Robert's eyes went hard and Eileen feared she'd made a fatal tactical error.

"If you're so keen on shooting them," Robert said to Patrick, "why don't you shoot them yourself."

Kyle seized the moment to stand with Patrick's gun in his grip, aiming at Robert.

"More than likely because I have his gun," Kyle said.

Pride flooded through Eileen. She'd never admired anyone's bravery more.

"Let's end this without incident," Kyle said. "Backup and law enforcement are on the way. Put down the gun and this is all over. I'm sure you have enough dirt on the higher-ups to plead out."

But Kyle's words didn't have the intended effect. Instead, Robert swung the gun wildly from where he'd maintained his aim on Eileen to Patrick.

He fired one shot, hitting his mark.

Kyle tackled Robert from behind and the two men hit the ground and rolled, scrambling for dominance, arms and legs entangled, flailing for position, fighting for control.

Patrick landed in a heap, no longer barking out orders, no longer saying a word. Blood seeped from beneath him and Eileen forgave herself for hoping he was dead.

Robert's gun fell from his grip, skittering across the dirt floor. Eileen scrambled for the weapon, wrapping her fingers around the cold metal and pushing to her feet.

The gun wobbled in her left hand as she moved in front of Jack's limp body, protecting him.

"Kyle," she called out. "Kyle."

Kyle maneuvered himself on top of Robert, gaining the upper hand. Robert's body went limp and if Eileen wasn't mistaken, she heard her older brother sob. He was a broken man who was about to lose every evil gain he'd made.

The chamber burst open, and Will and Martin barreled through, weapons drawn.

A rapid succession of emotions played out across their faces, and Eileen dropped to the floor next to Jack, feeling for a pulse.

Still there.

Still alive.

She'd found both brothers, yet her world would never be the same.

Will moved to Patrick and checked for a pulse,

then grimly shook his head. He studied Eileen and Jack and spoke quickly into his communicator.

"We need medical assistance and we need it now."

Kyle met Eileen's gaze and held it. "You okay?"

She nodded. "You?"

And then he spoke the simple statement she'd waited for, hoped for, prayed for these past four days.

"It's over."

EPILOGUE

Body Clock: 116:00 Status: Alive

Twenty-four hours later, Robert had made a full confession. In the end, he'd chosen family over greed, although he hadn't yet explained what had caused his sudden change of heart or why he'd killed Patrick in cold blood.

Had Patrick given one too many commands or made one too many requests? Or had Eileen's heartfelt plea reached Robert, breaking through the heart he'd thought long dead?

Perhaps Robert had decided to take vengeance for the parents the Caldwell children had never gotten a chance to know.

Eileen wasn't sure anyone would ever know what had transpired deep inside Robert's mind in the dank, dark room where Patrick had died and she and Jack had survived, but she wasn't sure she truly wanted to know.

Perhaps there were some questions to which it was

better not to know the answers.

Patrick's comments about her mother and Eileen's parentage fell into that same category. She'd given his words a lot of thought and decided she'd let them go. He knew her well enough to know unanswered questions ate at her. Had he spoken the cruel remarks intending them to erode away at her slowly?

In her heart, Eileen knew exactly who her mother and father were. And nothing Patrick O'Malley had said could shake that foundation.

She had no plans to give him the satisfaction.

Eileen hadn't set eyes on Robert since he'd been taken into custody, but she would.

This time she had no plans to run away. Not from Robert. Not from Jack. And not from their family's past.

Jack was expected to make a full recovery.

The doctors called his progress nothing short of miraculous, but Eileen knew the real reason for his improvement. He was on his way to the biggest prosecution of his career, and one he'd fought for not because of professional reasons, but for personal salvation.

With their mother's documentation and Robert's confession, Jack had enough to implicate DiMauro, Basso and Ferdinand King. Three giants of the typically invisible horror known as human trafficking were about to fall, and Eileen couldn't be more proud of her baby brother.

As for Eileen, she'd also found the key to her personal salvation. She had only to see her plans through.

She'd spent most of the past twenty-four hours by Jack's side, and only left him this morning to stop by the safe house and drive to the Caldwell farm.

While she'd never be able to change the Caldwell farm's past, she had the power to change its future.

Somehow she had a feeling her parents and grandparents would approve of her plans to rehab the house and gut the barn in order to build a good old-fashioned bed-and-breakfast. With hard work and elbow grease, she'd create a haven for those who needed an escape, who needed peace and quiet, who needed a place to rest or heal.

She'd done nothing but save her income during her time on Cielo and if she sold her foursquare and moved out to the farm, she'd have more than enough to see her plans to fruition.

For the first time in her life, she knew exactly where she belonged. Her Pittsburgh roots had finally pulled her home.

The one unanswered question was Kyle.

They hadn't spoken about the future or about the time they'd spent together.

Their lovemaking.

Their intimate talks.

Maggie had told Eileen the team planned to fly back to Seattle today, their work here done. Eileen had driven to the safe house after she'd left Jack, hoping to say her goodbyes, but Kyle had been gone without saying a word to anyone.

Eileen had called him on his cell phone, but had been able only to leave a message.

All she could do now was wait, and hope the man she'd fallen in love with would call her back, or show up at her door. Because of all the promises she'd made herself, one had become more important than the rest.

She planned to tell Kyle she loved him. And whether or not he returned the sentiment, Eileen would know she'd finally faced her darkest fear.

She'd know she'd not only faced her life, but also embraced it, if only for a little while.

KYLE PULLED his rental car to the side of the lane approaching the Caldwell family farm. He knew Eileen's nerves must still be on edge after her ordeal and the last thing he wanted to do was startle her.

He planned to approach the house—and Eileen—slowly. After all, what he was about to do might very well turn out to be the most important maneuver of his life.

He'd left the safe house late the night before, telling no one where he was going, not even Will. In the eighteen hours since, he'd traveled to the West Coast and back, wanting to turn in his notice on his apartment and visit the cemetery.

He'd decided to finally let go of Sally and the life they'd shared.

She, of all people, would have been the first to push him toward Eileen, to encourage him to open his heart and risk loving again. But for reasons Kyle couldn't explain, he felt compelled to visit her grave, to take her flowers one more time, to finally lay her to rest.

After all, he wasn't about to doubt or ignore his intuition. Never again.

He wasn't sure he'd ever be able to explain what had happened beside Sally's grave, and he wasn't sure he'd ever try. Perhaps he'd tell Eileen someday—when he was ready.

He knew no matter what he decided, Eileen would understand. Perhaps that was one of the reasons he'd fallen in love with her. She had an innate kindness and understanding that soothed his rough interior. They fit together, as if they'd been made for one another.

As Kyle had kneeled beside Sally's tombstone, the vision of the bank robbery and shooting had replayed once more, but this time, Kyle hadn't fought the images, hadn't shoved them from his mind.

He'd let the scenes play out, witnessing Sally's passage from this world to the next, fully at peace, never having felt a moment of pain.

The calm understanding that filled Kyle then filled him now as he walked toward Eileen's door, a brand-new toolbox hanging from his grip.

The front door of the farmhouse opened as he approached.

So much for quiet entrances.

The smile that lit Eileen's face filled Kyle with a joy he hadn't thought possible.

"You're not going with the team?" she asked, hope shining in her eyes.

Kyle stepped close, set the toolbox on the front step and pulled her into his arms, crushing her lips beneath his, tasting deeply of the woman he wanted to spend the rest of his life with.

He pulled back and searched her expression for any sign of doubt, any sign of disappointment that he was here, before her, heart in hand.

He saw none.

And then she did something so incredible Kyle knew every sleepless night, every vision, every moment of intuition and pain and loss he'd suffered in the past had been part of a master plan to bring him here, to this moment, to this woman.

"I love you."

Eileen spoke the words so softly Kyle was almost afraid he'd imagined them, but then she told him again, and again, as he pulled her into his arms and swung her into the air, ever mindful of the cast on her right arm.

Instead of setting her back on her feet, he bundled her into his arms and carried her across the threshold, into their new life together.

"I love you, too," he whispered, as he nuzzled a kiss to her neck, inhaling deeply of the fruity scent of her shampoo.

She pointed toward the gleaming silver toolbox left behind on the step. "Is that what I think it is?"

He nodded, a grin tugging at the corners of his mouth. "I heard you had this crazy idea about rehabbing this place. I figured the tools would make me useful, if nothing else."

She laughed then, the sound a wonderful melody of joy and promise that started low inside her, building in intensity.

A potent jolt of need and desire hit Kyle like a sucker punch and he headed for the staircase, never slowing to shut the front door.

"Kyle?" Eileen asked through happy laughter. "Where are we going?"

"Remember that last morning you sneaked out of bed?"

She nodded, a crooked smile pulling at her lips. She touched a fingertip to his bruised face. Her touch so gentle and full of love it sent a lightning bolt of heat straight to his center.

"Well," he continued, as he hit the top step and bee-lined toward the nearest bedroom, "there were a few things I still wanted to try."

"And now?"

"And now I intend to try them." He lowered her gently onto the bed and pressed a kiss to the hollow at the base of her throat. "Over and over and over again."

AND WHILE Kyle and Eileen began their new life together, the rest of The Body Hunters team boarded the jet back to Seattle, where they'd wait until a new case called.

When a new body clock began to tick, they'd go where they were needed. After all, that's what The Body Hunters did.

Don't miss these additional Body Hunters titles:

Gone
Silenced

ABOUT THE AUTHOR

USA Today and Wall Street Journal bestseller Kathleen Long is the author of nineteen novels in the genres of women's fiction, suspense, and fiction for young readers. A native of Wilmington, Delaware, and a graduate of the University of Delaware, she divides her time between suburban Philadelphia and the Jersey shore. When Kathleen is not hiding in the corner of the local library writing her next book, she spends her time bribing her teen to take off her headphones, begging the dog to heel, and teaching creative writing.

Please visit her at www.kathleenlong.com

BOOKS IN THIS SERIES

Body Hunters

If you love fast-paced romantic suspense, you'll devour the heart-pounding Body Hunters series from USA TODAY bestseller, Kathleen Long.

Gone

In a race against a killer, can two desperate parents save their daughter before time runs out?

The Body Clock is ticking.

Maggie Connor will do whatever it takes to find her missing daughter, but what if that means working alongside the husband she "buried" seventeen years earlier? In order to save his family, Will faked his own death, and he'll stop at nothing to bring his daughter home now. Maggie and Will's reunion ignites an undeniable anger—and an unmistakable passion—but will they find the killer before it's too late?

Silenced

Body Hunter Lily Christides never imagined she'd one day be chasing her sister's killer. But when investigative reporter Nicole Christides is murdered shortly after helping overturn a killer's sentence, that's exactly where Lily finds herself.

Philadelphia detective Cameron Hughes never dreamed the man he worked so hard to convict would one day walk free. When Nicole Christides is found murdered, Cam is determined to put Buddy Grey back where he belongs. Behind bars.

Lily believes Grey is innocent. Cam plans to prove his guilt.

When the killer makes it known Lily is next on his list, she and Cam begin a race against the clock. Will they unmask the murderer before time runs out? Or will the truth be silenced forever?

Shattered

When hotel manager Eileen Caldwell leaves Isle de Cielo to return to the life she left behind, she never imagined she'd walk into her past. Literally. After working to escape the mystery of her older brother's disappearance and suicide, she now finds herself searching again, this time for her younger brother, vanished in exactly the same way. Has history repeated itself? Or is there time to save this life, avoiding the outcome that's haunted her dreams—and nightmares—for the past five years?

Kyle Landenburg has tried to forget the hotel manager who turned his head during the Body Hunters' Cielo investigation. Blaming himself for the death of the only woman he ever loved, he's vowed never to let his emotions again be vulnerable, yet he hasn't been able to shake the impact Eileen Caldwell blazed across his memory and his heart.

When the Body Hunters take on the case of her missing brother, he'll use his intuition and skills to do whatever it takes to bring the man home alive. But when the past turns out to be far more complicated than anyone ever imagined and the present becomes a maze of dead-end clues and life-threatening twists, he'll be fighting more than the romantic tension building between him and Eileen. He'll be fighting an invisible foe determined that this time Eileen's family will be shattered...forever.